The Haunting
by

Kathi Daley

I want to thank the very talented Jessica Fischer for the cover art.

I so appreciate Bruce Curran, who is always ready and willing to answer my cyber questions, Jayme Maness, who helps out with my book clubs and special events, and Peggy Hyndman, for helping sleuth out those pesky typos.

And, of course, thanks to the readers and bloggers in my life, who make doing what I do possible.

Thank you to Randy Ladenheim-Gil for the editing.

And finally I want to thank my sister Christy for always lending an ear and my husband Ken for allowing me time to write by taking care of everything else.

Books by Kathi Daley

Zoe Donovan Cozy Mystery:

Halloween Hijinks
The Trouble With Turkeys
Christmas Crazy
Cupid's Curse
Big Bunny Bump-off
Beach Blanket Barbie
Maui Madness
Derby Divas
Haunted Hamlet
Turkeys, Tuxes, and Tabbies
Christmas Cozy
Alaskan Alliance
Matrimony Meltdown
Soul Surrender
Heavenly Honeymoon
Hopscotch Homicide
Ghostly Graveyard
Santa Sleuth
Shamrock Shenanigans
Kitten Kaboodle
Costume Catastrophe
Candy Cane Caper
Holiday Hangover
Easter Escapade
Camp Carter
Trick or Treason
Reindeer Roundup – *December 2017*

Zimmerman Academy The New Normal
Ashton Falls Cozy Cookbook

Tj Jensen Paradise Lake Mysteries by Henery Press

Pumpkins in Paradise
Snowmen in Paradise
Bikinis in Paradise
Christmas in Paradise
Puppies in Paradise
Halloween in Paradise
Treasure in Paradise
Fireworks in Paradise – *October 2017*

Whales and Tails Cozy Mystery:
Romeow and Juliet
The Mad Catter
Grimm's Furry Tail
Much Ado About Felines
Legend of Tabby Hollow
Cat of Christmas Past
A Tale of Two Tabbies
The Great Catsby
Count Catula
The Cat of Christmas Present
A Winter's Tail
Taming of the Tabby
Frankencat
The Cat of Christmas Future – *November* 2017
The Cat of New Orleans – *February 2018*

Seacliff High Mystery:

The Secret
The Curse
The Relic
The Conspiracy
The Grudge
The Shadow
The Haunting

Sand and Sea Hawaiian Mystery:
Murder at Dolphin Bay
Murder at Sunrise Beach
Murder at the Witching Hour
Murder at Christmas
Murder at Turtle Cove
Murder at Water's Edge
Murder at Midnight – *October 2017*

Rescue Alaska Paranormal Mystery:
Finding Justice – *November 2017*

A Tess and Tilly Mystery:
The Christmas Letter – *December 2017*

Road to Christmas Romance:
Road to Christmas Past

Writers' Retreat Southern Mystery:
First Case
Second Look
Third Strike
Fourth Victim – *October 2017*

Chapter 1

Thursday, October 19

My life is a lie. Everything about me—my name, my past, even my future—is shrouded in secrets and half-truths. At my core, I'm basically an honest person, so it pains me that I must deceive the people I care about the most. My birth name is Amanda Parker. Prior to my death and very public funeral, I was a popular student, heiress to millions, and a well-known socialite. Only a handful of people in the entire world know that my death was staged to protect me from the men who threatened to kill me. When Amanda Parker died, Alyson Prescott was born.

As far as names go, I'm rather fond of Alyson, but after more than a year in witness protection, I find the line separating Amanda from Alyson has begun to blur. Despite the insanity that has become my life, I was dealing with the changes, until five months ago, when my handler whisked me away from my new life after an unconfirmed tip threatened my very existence.

Four months ago, my mother and I made the decision to return to Cutter's Cove, Oregon, despite the danger that may exist. The nightmares, which would come to overshadow my life, began the very next day. Although the intensity of the dream has escalated over time, the script for each dream is the same. I'm standing on the porch of a dilapidated old house looking at a dark-colored door. I instinctively know that my destiny resides beyond the threshold, but I'm paralyzed with fear and hesitant to enter. I gather my courage and fight the instinct to flee as I cautiously turn the handle and take a step inside. In the instant before I wake, I experience the terror and helplessness that has come to dominate even my waking hours.

"Earth to Alyson," my best friend Mackenzie Reynolds said as she snapped her fingers in front of my face.

I glanced at her, dazed, as I wondered where I was and why I was there.

"Class is over," Mac informed me. "We need to go."

"Was I sleeping?" I asked.

"I'm not sure. Your eyes were open, but you certainly didn't seem to be listening to the lecture."

"Did I drool?" I wiped the side of my mouth with one hand.

"Just a little. Don't worry; you didn't snore. I don't think anyone else knew you'd dozed off. That's the third time in a week. Are you okay?"

"Yeah," I said as I closed my book and slipped it into my backpack. "I just haven't been sleeping well. I guess everything is catching up with me."

"Still having the dream?"

I nodded. "Almost every night."

I slipped out of my desk and followed Mac out the door and into the crowded hallway of Seacliff High. Only one more period until lunch, when I could head to the library, find a table in the back, and have a proper nap.

"Do you think maybe you should talk to someone about what's going on?" Mac asked.

"Who would I talk to? We both know the dreams began after I returned to Cutter's Cove from Madrona Island. We both know the root of the dream stems from the fact that very bad men are trying to kill me and I have no idea whether they've actually found me and are waiting for the right opportunity to strike, or if Donovan's intel is wrong and my cover is secure."

Mac stopped walking. She turned to look at me, her dark eyes mirroring her concern. "I know this is a crazy way to live and I can't imagine how difficult this must be for you. You know I missed you desperately when you were away, but are you certain coming back to Cutter's Cove was the right decision?"

"Honestly?" I tilted my head to one side, causing my long blond hair to cascade over my shoulder. "I'm not sure. I do know that unless I want to run forever, at some point I need to make a stand."

Mac took my hand in hers and continued down the hall. "You know I'm here for you. Whatever you need."

"I may need to copy your history notes."

"You got it. In fact, why don't we get together after school and I'll help you study for tomorrow's exam?"

"There's an exam tomorrow?"

"Midterm. Remember, we were given a study guide on Monday."

"Oh, that exam." I groaned. I had to admit it was beginning to feel like I actually was losing my mind. "I do need to study, but I promised Caleb I'd go over to the house the Halloween committee has selected for the Haunted Hayride to see if I can get a sense about what's going on."

"Is weird stuff still happening?" Mac asked.

"The weirdest."

"Poor Caleb."

Caleb Wellington was the event chairperson for the Haunted Hayride and he took his responsibilities to the school and the town very seriously. "Not only are there all sorts of strange sounds and slamming doors, but some of the props were moved from one location to another, and there's been a fair amount of vandalism as well. Based on what Caleb has told me, I'm going to go out on a limb and say the house really is haunted."

Mac furrowed her brow. "Can ghosts do that? Move things?"

"As far as I know, no. In my experience to date ghosts aren't corporeal and can't move things, but things are being moved and there doesn't seem to be an earthly explanation, so for the time being I'm going to suspend disbelief and see what I can discover. Caleb is a smart guy and he's pretty much convinced the problems they've been having are paranormal in nature."

"Even if that's true and ghosts are behind all the problems, is there anything you can do about it?"

I shrugged. "I'm not sure. If the house is haunted I'll need to see if I can determine why the spirits are hanging around. If I know why they failed to move on maybe I can find a way to help them resolve their issues. And if I can't do that maybe I can at least find a way to appease them so they'll quit messing with Caleb's props. I don't suppose you'd want to come with me?"

Mac looped her arm though mine as we continued down the hallway. "You know I will. And I'm sure Trevor will come as well if he doesn't have football, although he did say something about extralong practice sessions this week because there's a home game tomorrow." Mac had referred to Trevor Johnson, the third member of our awesome threesome. "I have next period with him, so I'll ask him. Do you want to meet for lunch?"

"I'm going to head to the library instead. Tell Trevor I'll meet him in the parking lot after school. If he has football ask him to text me. Either way, I'll swing by and pick you up from your internship on my way out to the house." Mac was a computer genius who worked for a software company as an intern during fifth and sixth periods.

A look of concern crossed Mac's face. "Are you sure you don't want to have lunch with us? You're looking a little thin."

"I'm sure. I have a granola bar in my backpack. I'll nibble on it between classes, but right now my body is demanding sleep over food."

"Okay. I'll see you after school. And maybe we can study after we check out the haunted house. I have a feeling this midterm is going to be a tough one."

"I need to study and I need to pass that class. Why don't you plan to come over for dinner? Trevor too. I'll text my mom to tell her to expect you."

"That sounds good."

Somehow I managed to stay awake through my fourth period computer science class and was looking forward to a power nap in the library. I'd been spending my lunch hour napping more and more often lately, and I was sure someone was going to notice and say something at some point. When that happened I guess I'd have to alter my routine and maybe nap in my car, but for now the library provided a warm, quiet place to catch some Z's.

The library at Seacliff High was actually a pretty awesome place to hang out even when you weren't looking for a place to nap. The room was quaint and cozy, with two levels, each containing mahogany bookshelves and hardwood tables and chairs. The ceiling was high in the center of the building, allowing for the levels to be open to each other. I'd settled in on the second floor at a table in the back that provided the best place to nap unnoticed. I took my sweater out of my backpack, folded it to use it for a pillow, and lay my head down on the table in front of me.

"Alyson," I heard Chelsea Green say just as I was drifting into unconsciousness.

I opened one eye but didn't lift my head from where it was resting. "Yes?"

"Are you okay? You haven't shown up in the lunchroom all week."

Chelsea and I weren't all that close, so I was surprised she'd noticed. It wasn't that we didn't get along; it was more that she was an A-list cheerleader and I was a no-list weirdo who saw ghosts and solved mysteries. "I'm fine. Just a little tired. Did you need something?"

Chelsea sat down on a chair across from me. I groaned as I opened my other eye and raised my head. It looked like I wasn't going to be able to avoid finding out what was on Chelsea's mind no matter how much I really wanted to drift into a dreamless sleep.

"Because you're awake anyway I do have a teensy problem I could use your help with." Chelsea tilted her head so her long dark hair brushed the table as she spoke.

"And what teensy problem might that be?"

"I have a stalker."

"A stalker?"

"For the past couple of weeks someone has been sending me photos. They've been taken in different locations, but all of them are of me during the day. At first I just thought it was one of my so-called friends pulling a prank, but now I'm not so sure."

"These photos—were they taken at school?"

"Yes, initially, either at school, at cheerleading practice, or at a school-related event. But lately I've been receiving photos taken at home, the most recent at my dad's birthday dinner two nights ago. It's really beginning to irritate me."

I sat up straighter. "Have you told anyone else what you told me?"

Chelsea shook her head. "I'm not sure who I can trust. The photos have to have been taken by someone who knows me well enough to know my routine. And they've been sent to me by both text and personal email, which means they also know my phone number and email address."

I narrowed my gaze. "Are any of the photos inappropriate?"

"Not really. There were a few without makeup, which terrified me, but so far, I haven't been sent any photos of me getting dressed or in the shower. Still, I'm starting to feel violated. I find myself looking over my shoulder all the time. It's creepy."

"I agree; it is creepy. You should tell your parents. Or maybe even the police."

Chelsea crossed her arms across her chest. "No. I can't do that. If I tell my parents they'll probably keep me under lock and key until they find out who's behind the photos, and if I tell the cops they'll interrogate all my friends. For all I know, this really is just some joke, and I don't want to look like I give a rat's ass if it's just one of my stupid friends pulling a prank. If it got out that I ran to my parents over a joke it would destroy my popularity ranking. What I need is for someone like you, who likes to play Nancy Drew, to look into this quietly."

I paused but didn't answer.

"Please. I can pay you."

I frowned. "I don't want your money, but I'm worried. Being stalked is nothing to take lightly. The person behind the photos could be dangerous."

"Maybe, or it could just be Cora Lee trying to make me look like an idiot. You know she was mad when I beat her out for homecoming queen. It would be just like her to come up with a lame prank to embarrass me."

I frowned as I considered Chelsea's request. While having a stalker was serious business, Chelsea was a self-serving snob who was both the most popular girl in school and one of the most hated. I could totally see someone sending her the photos just to mess with her. If it was just a prank and she let it be known that the photos had gotten to her I did see how it could affect the way she was perceived by others; she was famous for trying to pretend she didn't care in the least when others tried to retaliate against her for one slight or another.

"Please, Alyson. I'll be nice to you and everything."

I raised an eyebrow. "Don't do me any favors."

"Okay, then, I'll totally ignore you if that's what you want. You're the only one who can help me with this."

"Okay," I eventually said. "I'll look in to it, but I have some conditions."

"Such as?"

"You show me all the photos you've received so far as well as all you receive in the future. If I suspect at any point you're in actual danger we tell your parents what's going on."

Chelsea paused and then answered, "Okay. I guess I can live with that."

"I'll also need to bring Mac in on this. I know she isn't your favorite person, but she can help us track down the origin of the texts and emails."

Chelsea let out a loud sigh. "Oh, all right. But no one else."

"I can't guarantee Trevor won't find out. The three of us are a team. We spend a lot of time together, he's helped in the past, and quite frankly, it will make it easier for me if I don't have to keep it from him. Besides, if your stalker is male he might have a better chance of getting a confession, if we even get that far."

Chelsea hesitated.

"You know Trevor cares about you, and you know he can keep a secret."

Chelsea groaned. "Oh, okay. You can bring Mac and Trevor in it, but that's it. If you need to bring my name into a conversation with anyone else I need you to promise you'll check with me first."

"Agreed."

Chelsea smiled. "Great. So where do we start?"

I jotted down my email address and slipped it across the table to Chelsea. "Forward the photos to my personal email, not my school one. Once I get them I'll talk things over with Mac and we'll come up with a strategy. The easiest way to figure out who's doing this to you will probably be to backtrack the photos to the phone number the texts were sent from or the IP address the emails were sent from."

"Okay, I'll do it after school, and thanks, Alyson. I know I haven't always been nice to you, so I do appreciate your helping me."

"No problem."

I started to lay my head back down when Chelsea spoke once again. "You know, you're looking a little ragged. If you aren't going to get the sleep you need some concealer would be a good idea. The dark circles under your eyes are going to begin to attract attention and I sense attention isn't what you're after."

Chelsea was right about that. Attention wasn't at all what I was after. "Thanks. I'll keep your suggestion in mind. Now if we're done…"

"Certainly."

Chelsea stood up and I lay my head back down on the desk. Unfortunately, the bell for fifth period rang before I had a chance to even close my eyes. Despite how desperately I needed it, it looked like I wasn't going to get my power nap after all.

Chapter 2

The Haunted Hayride was put on every year by Seacliff High's drama department. Last year it had been held at the Thomases' farm, but this year the committee needed to look for a new location because the farm had been sold. After weeks of searching Caleb had managed to find another house that not only had been deserted for years but was situated in the middle of a dense forest that would work perfectly for the Hayride. The only problem was, the house really seemed to be haunted, and the resident haunts didn't seem to want to be disturbed.

Trevor did text to let me know he'd have an extended practice that afternoon, so I headed to the software firm where Mac did her internship. She was not only a computer genius, she was a genius overall, and I couldn't help but feel saddened by the fact that in less than a year she'd be going off to some Ivy League college while I stayed behind in Cutter's Cove, hiding from the men who wanted to kill me.

"You look happy," I commented as Mac slipped into the passenger seat of my Jeep.

"I am. My boss finally assigned me my own project."

"That's awesome. I know you've been wanting to get out from under the shadow of the paid employees. What are you going to be working on?"

"It's a game called Zombie Invasion. I know it isn't anything that will change technology as we know it, but it's a start. Having my own project is going to look good on my college applications too."

"Well, congratulations. I'm sure your game will be awesome."

"I hope so. I want to create something unique, even if it's mostly going to feature flesh eating, entrails feasting, and organ dining."

I wrinkled my nose. "Sounds pretty gross."

"Oh, it will be," Mac said with enthusiasm. "The grossest and goriest I can possibly make it. And I'm going to make it totally lifelike."

"Sounds..." I wanted to be supportive, but it sounded awful.

"While zombies eating humans wouldn't have been my project of choice, it's still a good opportunity for me," Mac continued. "I've already got a bunch of ideas on how to improve the graphics. It's going to be bloody, but it's also going to be totally awesome."

"If you say so." I grimaced.

Mac's smile faded. "You look tired. Didn't you get your power nap today?"

"I tried, but Chelsea interrupted me just as I was drifting off. She has a problem she needs our help with."

"What kind of problem?"

"She has a stalker."

Mac frowned. "A stalker?"

I shared with her what Chelsea had told me.

"It sounds like she should call the cops," Mac said. "A stalker can be dangerous."

"I told her the same thing, but she's so concerned about her parents flipping out or being embarrassed by it that she'd rather take her chances with us. She did agree to talk to them about what's going on if we find out anything that makes it seem like she might be in real danger. Do I need to turn left or right on the coast road?"

"Left. After about a mile you'll turn left again onto Harbinger Lane. That turns into a dirt road that dead ends at the house. I spoke to Caleb earlier and he said he and some of the other volunteers would be at the house trying to repair the damage that's been done the past few days."

"At first, I thought Caleb really might have ghosts, which was why I agreed to come out in the first place, but I spoke to one of the volunteers during fifth period, who told me the extent of the damage that's been caused. Not only have things been moved, but there's graffiti on the walls and some of the props were hacked up into little pieces. If you ask me, causing that much damage to school property sounds more like a student thing than a ghost thing."

"Yeah. I agree, but I suppose eliminating the spook angle will help him focus in on the real prankster. Harbinger Lane is just on the other side of the big grove of trees."

I looked to where Mac was pointing to a grove of aspens decked out in fall color. I turned onto the road and slowed down. There were a few driveways connecting to the road on both the left and the right. They were long drives I assumed led to other farms. Once the paved road turned into a dirt lane I slowed down even more so as not to kick up too much dust. There were five cars parked in front of a large but dilapidated house. I parked well away from the others so I wouldn't get blocked in if other volunteers arrived. Then I turned off the ignition and Mac and I climbed out.

She paused and looked at the house. "I'll admit this house has a spooky feel to it."

"It really does." I nodded. "And with the forest all around, it seems a lot more isolated than it actually is. Caleb told me he was able to arrange parking at a dirt lot about a mile from here. He plans to have the wagons begin the route there and then drop people off at the house for the party."

"It sounds like he has it handled, although I don't see how it's going to beat last year's hayride."

"Last year really was pretty spectacular," I agreed.

"It looks like they've begun to set up the fake cemetery. Did you buy a headstone this year?" Mac asked.

"Not yet, but I will."

In the past, the volunteers had just made up epitaphs to write on the wooden headstones, but Caleb had come up with the idea of selling the headstones, which would be decorated with custom inscriptions as an additional fund-raiser. The idea had earned the drama department an additional five hundred dollars so far.

Mac and I carefully climbed the four steps to the front door. When we walked in we found two volunteers painting a wall that had been vandalized when someone painted pictures of dragons in red. I was certain those drawings weren't the work of a ghost, but I did sense an otherworldly presence, though I hadn't come across any ghosts yet.

"Is Caleb around?" I asked.

"Upstairs," a girl with dark hair who I seemed to remember from the spring musical last year answered.

"Okay, thanks," I said as I headed up the stairs, with Mac following close behind.

The stairway led to a landing that connected hallways to the left and the right. I could hear people talking on the left, so I headed in that direction. I found Caleb speaking to a volunteer. They paused their conversation when Mac and I walked into a room that looked as if it might have been used as an office or perhaps a library.

"Oh good, you made it," Caleb greeted us. "What do you think? Do we have actual ghosts?"

I frowned. "I'm not sure. If it's okay with you, Mac and I will look around. We'll find you when we're done."

Caleb shrugged. "Fine by me. The main living area is on the first floor. There are bedrooms, offices, and bathrooms on this floor, and there's both an attic and a cellar."

"It's a big house."

"Over five thousand square feet if you count the attic and cellar. One of the reasons I was interested in this property was its size. I love the fact that there are so many rooms that can be used to create microenvironments within the larger overall theme. If you have any questions or need anything just holler; otherwise I'll leave you to do your thing."

"Thanks." I glanced at Mac. "Should we start in the attic and work our way down?"

"I'm just following you."

The stairs to the attic were steep and narrow. I imagined Caleb planned to have the house fairly dark on the night of the party, so I hoped he hadn't planned to utilize the attic because I could almost see an accident in the making. The door separating the landing at the top of the stairs from the large A-shaped room groaned as Mac and I pushed it open. The dank and dusty attic contained remnants from residents past, including old pieces of furniture, boxes stacked one atop another, and several dressmaker's mannequins with dresses still draped over them.

"I wonder why the previous owner left all this stuff behind," Mac mused.

"I suppose it's is possible whoever used to own the house died and the heir hasn't gotten around to sorting through the stuff that was left up here, although the rest of the house was cleaned out. We can ask Caleb about the history of the house. Knowing who lived here could help us identify our ghost, if there is one."

"Do you see anyone?" Mac asked.

I shook my head. "It appears the attic is ghost free. At least for the moment." I took several steps into the room, studying the floor as I walked. "Someone has been in here, though. Based on the size of the footprints I'm going to say a small someone."

"A child?"

"Probably." I bent down and looked at the footprints more closely. "It looks like there are three different sets of prints. All made by tennis shoes. All too small to belong to an adult, unless it was a really small adult." I stood back up and looked around. "Chances are Caleb's spooks are kids."

"Caleb mentioned that he locks all the doors and windows when he leaves every day. And he said everything's still locked tight when he gets here the next day. If the pranksters are human children instead of ghosts how are they getting in and out?"

"Let's keep our eye out for a way in while we're looking around."

After we finished looking around the attic, Mac and I tackled the second floor. There were six bedrooms, two baths, and the large room where we'd first found Caleb that I'd imagined may have been an office, although whatever had been in the room before had been removed. It appeared the second floor was free of ghosts as well, so we headed down to the main floor, where Caleb, along with five other volunteers, were hanging cobwebs and draping the walls with black fabric.

"Did you find anything?" Caleb asked.

I shook my head. "Not so far, but I found footprints in the attic. Ghosts don't leave footprints, so I'm going out on a limb and suggesting you have human pranksters messing with your props. My guess is they're kids maybe between eight and twelve, based on the size of the shoeprints."

Caleb frowned. "If kids are getting in I'd sure like to know how. I check and recheck all the locks when I leave."

"I suppose it's possible there's a hidden entry of some sort. This is an old house, and the old houses in this area, especially the larger ones near the sea, tend to have hidden passageways. We'll keep an eye out for something like that. We'll finish looking around on this floor and then go down to the cellar."

"I hadn't thought of that, but you make a good point," Caleb responded. "The history center is full of old photos and artifacts from back in the day when men involved in illegal trade lived here." Caleb paused and then continued. "The staircase down to the cellar opens into the kitchen just beyond the pantry. You'll see a doorway. I wasn't planning to use the cellar for the party so I haven't spent much time down there, but I remember there being cabinets along the back wall. If there's a hidden passage I'd start by looking there."

"Thanks, we will," I said.

The first floor of the house had undergone the greatest amount of decorating, so I assumed the volunteers had spent most of their time there. The rooms we explored didn't reveal any signs of ghosts, so Mac and I went downstairs to the cellar. When we arrived in the cold and damp room I was overcome with a feeling of sorrow.

"Do you see anything?" Mac asked as I stood in the middle of the room and looked around.

I turned slowly in a circle to get a panoramic view. "No. I don't see anything, but I definitely feel something."

Mac took a step closer to me. "Like what?"

I placed a hand on my chest. "A profound sadness mingled with fear and confusion. I think if the house does have ghosts we'll find them down here."

"Sounds like the ghosts aren't in a good place."

"Ghosts rarely are, but this seems more intense. I can almost feel the emotion that fills the space, but there's something else as well."

"Something else? Like what?"

I frowned. "I'm not sure. I sense the cellar is home to more than one spirit. I also sense that the spirits are in some way related to each other."

"Related as in a parent and child or siblings?"

I narrowed my gaze. "Maybe, but not necessarily. The spirits who reside here are linked, but I'm not picking up a genetic link. They may have died here together or they may have died at different times but were killed by the same person."

"So you think they were murdered?"

"That would be my guess at this point. I'd like to make contact. Maybe if I can I'll be able to figure out who the spirits belonged to and how to help them. My suspicion, however, is that our ghostly friends are hiding out while all the people are here." I paused to consider the situation. "Everything that's been happening seems to happen at night. I think I might come back after everyone's gone."

"History midterm," Mac reminded me.

"Oh yeah. I do want to pass that. Maybe tomorrow night, after the game."

"You seriously want to come back here after dark?"

I nodded. "I think if we want answers that's when we'll find them." I glanced at Mac. "You in?"

"Visiting a spooky old house after dark that's very likely haunted by actual ghosts? Sure!" Mac screeched with a tone of panic in her voice. "Who wouldn't want to do something crazy like that?"

"I can come alone. Or maybe Trevor will want to come with me."

"I'll come," Mac grumbled. "But let's ask Trevor anyway. And bring Tucker. I think a haunted house is the perfect place to have a big, protective German shepherd on hand."

"Great." I smiled. "I'll arrange it with Caleb."

I chatted with Caleb to make arrangements to return the following evening, then Mac and I headed to the house I share with my mother on a bluff overlooking the sea. When Mom and I moved to Cutter's Cove one of the things that really sold us on this specific location was the huge, dilapidated mansion that was a total mess but was situated right on the water. Mom and I had spent a year remodeling and now we had a warm, comfortable home with fantastic views on a very private plot of land at the end of its own road.

Mom must have seen us coming because the front door magically opened when I pulled up and my dog, Tucker, came running out to greet us. One of the things I love the most about my big bundle of joy is that he's always so happy to see me, no matter how long I've been gone. I bent down to pet my pup as he performed his happy dance at my feet before trotting over to Mac and giving her the same hero's welcome.

"I wish my mom would let me have a dog." Mac laughed as Tucker licked her face. "It must be so nice to have someone greet you with such enthusiasm every day."

"He is pretty great. I don't know what I'd do without him. When I had to leave without notice last spring it was Tucker who gave me the courage to do what I needed to do it."

Mac and I headed inside and greeted my mom, who was busy making homemade seafood chowder, which she planned to serve with a crisp green salad and fresh-from-the-bakery sourdough bread. I noticed chocolate cake on the counter, which I knew was Trevor's favorite.

"Isn't Trevor coming too?" Mom asked, confirming my suspicion that she'd made the cake just for him.

"Yeah, he should be here any time." I crossed the room and picked up Shadow, a new animal spirit in my life, who I'd connected with while visiting Madrona Island. Shadow was a large black cat with thick long hair who seemed to be able to see ghosts the same way I could. I'd noticed Tucker was completely unaware of the ghosts that visited our house, but Shadow seemed to know they were nearby even before I did. Maybe I'd bring both Shadow and Tucker with me when Mac and I went back to the haunted house tomorrow evening.

Trevor arrived shortly after Mac and I went up to my room to study. He was interested in what we'd found at the house, so we filled him in on the footprints in the attic, the feeling of ghostly presence in the cellar, and our plans to go back the next evening. I also shared the history of the house Caleb had told us before we left.

"The last person to live in the house was a man named Eliston Weston. He died in the house two years ago. Caleb said Mr. Weston owned the house for about thirty years after buying it from a couple who'd used it to take in foster kids. He wasn't certain why the couple, Joe and Jenny Jenkins, sold the property to Mr. Weston, but as far as he knew, no deaths had occurred while they lived there. Prior to the Jenkinses, a farmer named Walter Bentley lived in the house with his wife and four children. Caleb's pretty sure Mr. Bentley inherited the farm from his father, but he didn't know if there were other owners before that."

"If the ghosts you sensed do reside in the house does it mean they died there?" Trevor asked.

"Not necessarily," I answered, "but ghosts are most likely found in places that have meaning for them. Where they died or perhaps where they lived while alive. Based on what Caleb told me, my first guess was that we're dealing with Mr. Weston's ghost, although my sense is that our ghosts were murdered, and Caleb said he was pretty sure he died of natural causes. I can't know for certain who or what we're dealing with until I make contact, which I hope to do tomorrow night. You in?"

"I'm in," Trevor said. "Should we head over right after the game?"

"There isn't any reason to show up before Caleb and his volunteers are done for the day. The game is at five, so you should be done by eight. We'll grab a bite to eat and then go over."

Chapter 3

Friday, October 20

Thanks to Mac's help the previous evening, and the fact that I'd stayed up late studying, I managed not only to pass my history exam but to do fairly well. A bonus to the late night of studying was total exhaustion and a dreamless sleep, providing relief from the nightmare for the first time in weeks. Four hours of uninterrupted sleep did wonders for my mood and energy level, so it was a happy and alert Alyson who met Mac in the library during lunch hour to work on Chelsea's stalker problem.

"I looked at all the photos Chelsea forwarded to me," I informed Mac. "None of them seem threatening in nature and so far, the photographer hasn't crossed the line into the perverted. The settings where the photos are being taken are getting bolder. Initially, all the photos were at school or of school-related activities, but the more recent ones were taken while Chelsea was at home."

Mac studied the information I'd given her. "It looks like the emails were sent from several different computers, which is a little odd, but all the computers are at the school."

"Do you know which computers?" I asked.

"Not offhand, but I can find out."

"Okay, what about the email addresses the photos were sent from?"

"They were all sent from student email accounts, but from different ones."

I frowned. "You mean Chelsea has more than one stalker?"

"No, probably not. What I'm saying is that the stalker has access to multiple student accounts and is using a different one each time a photo is sent."

"But how? Every time you send an email from your account you need to log in with your student ID and personal password."

Mac bit her lip as she studied the screen. "Either the stalker is a highly skilled hacker or has access to that information. My money's on the latter, although if I wanted to, with enough time and the right equipment, I could hack into the student accounts. I'm not sure there's anyone else at school with the skill level to do that, however, and no, I'm not the stalker."

I laughed. "It never occurred to me that you could be. Not only do I trust your integrity but I know for a fact that you wouldn't want to spend that much time following Chelsea around. If the stalker has access to the student IDs and passwords it must be a staff member."

"Perhaps, although the thought of that has escalated things on the creep-o-meter by quite a lot."

I felt a shiver crawl up my spine. An adult stalker was a whole other ball game as far as I was concerned. "Is there a way to find out who might have accessed this information?"

Mac tilted her head. "Perhaps. I can look around a bit, but it's going to take longer than we have right now."

"Okay, so what about the texts? They all look to have been sent from the same phone number. Maybe we can trace that more easily than the emails."

Mac turned in her chair and began typing commands into her laptop. "Does Chelsea have any idea why her stalker has been spending what appears to be an enormous amount of time following her around?"

"She doesn't know. So far there haven't been any threats or demands associated with the photos. In fact, Chelsea said there hasn't been any correspondence at all other than the photos. If I had to guess I'd say the photographer is working up to something."

"What do you mean?"

"At this point the stalker is simply establishing the fact that Chelsea can never know when she's being watched. Whoever it is wants her to feel exposed and vulnerable, and it seems to be working. Chelsea told me she's taken to keeping her bedroom blinds closed at all times, but that hasn't stopped the photographer from taking photos of her in other rooms of her house." I sorted through the photos and pulled one up. "See, here she is at the dining table with her parents. The front of the house is clearly visible as well, so the photograph had to have been taken from a vantage point outside the window. The photographer could have been in her yard, but it seems more likely he was across the street or in a parked car on the street. The photo is of good quality, so I'm going to guess the photographer has a professional camera and a very expensive telephoto lens. There's no way these photos were taken with a cell phone or some small portable camera."

Mac studied the photo. "Even if this was taken from a car the photos taken of her on campus would have to have been taken from a nearby location. It seems a person carrying around some huge camera would stand out. I wonder if we ask around if someone will remember seeing someone at school or near Chelsea's house with a camera like that."

I continued to sort through the photos I'd printed out, dividing them into piles based on location. "I guess it couldn't hurt to try. Unless you can trace the cell, which will lead us to the person who forwarded the photos to Chelsea. Now that the idea's in my head that the stalker could be a member of the staff I think I'm going to talk to Chelsea again about telling her parents what's going on."

"I agree with you, but knowing Chelsea, she won't want to go there unless she has to. Her dad is a town council member and her mother is involved in a lot of charities. They both have social standing, and I can see that she wouldn't want her situation to become common knowledge. Besides, maybe Chelsea knows more about what's going on than she told you. Maybe she suspects who the stalker is and just wants us to prove it."

"You think so?"

Mac lifted one shoulder. "I don't know for certain, but if someone was following me around I'd be majorly concerned. Chelsea just seems to see the whole thing as an annoyance."

I considered that. "When I spoke to her she tried to put on a brave face, but I could see she was scared. I didn't get the feeling she had any idea who was behind the photos. If she did she'd most likely handle it herself rather than ask for a favor from me."

"Yeah, I guess that's a good point." Mac continued to work at the computer while we spoke. Eventually, she sat back and looked at me. "I have good news and bad news."

"Okay. What's the bad news?"

"The texts were sent from an unregistered burner cell."

"And the good news?"

"If given enough time I may be able to track down where the cell was purchased, and if we can isolate the right information, we may be able to track it back to the person who purchased it. Unless, of course, they paid cash, and most stores don't keep records of cash transactions. Either way, I'll need better equipment than my laptop to do it. I'll try to find time while I'm at my internship, which I really need to get to."

"Okay. Thanks, Mac. I'll pick you up after school and we'll go to the game together."

******

The Seacliff High Pirates were currently tied for first place in their division. If they managed to secure first place they'd be in the state finals for the second year in a row. Trevor was the star quarterback for the team and, as such, a candidate for Chelsea's unwanted affection. I used to think her pursuit of Trevor was based on deeply felt personal emotion, but I'd come to realize that the object of her desire was more often than not whoever was on top of the Seacliff High social hierarchy at any given moment. Unlike a lot of jocks, Trevor didn't seem to care about being überpopular. In fact, he didn't seem to care what people thought about him one way or another. Still, his skill as a football player, combined with his boy-next-door good looks and his total disregard for social standing seemed to make him all that more desirable to the female students at school.

As head cheerleader, Chelsea was busy getting ready for the big game, so I decided to try to track her down when the game was over but before Trevor, Mac, and I headed to the haunted house for our meet and greet with the resident spooks. At least I hoped it was a meet and greet. I had sensed the presence of at least one spirit but suspected there were two or more. I just hoped that most of the decorating crew had vacated the premises by the time we arrived so the ghosts would come out of hiding and make themselves known.

"I want to grab a corn dog if you'll get us seats," Mac said after we paid for our tickets and entered through the front gate of the football stadium.

"Okay. I'll head for our usual section."

"Do you want anything from the snack bar?"

"Maybe just a Diet Coke. If I can't get our usual seats I'll have to see what else I can find. If I have to move I'll text you where I am."

"Okay, great. Hopefully we're here early enough to beat the crowd."

It was more than an hour until game time, but the stands were already almost a quarter of the way full. I knew from experience that by kickoff it would be standing room only. This was a big game against the competitor with whom we were tied for first and today could very well determine the likelihood of the Pirates being division champs. I knew Trevor was both excited and nervous and hoped with all my heart that he and the team would have a winning game that would move them to the number one spot alone.

Luckily, the seats Mac and I preferred, at the top of the bleachers and away from the cheerleaders, were still available, so I slipped into one and set my jacket on another. The air was crisp and cool now that autumn had officially descended upon us. The hill behind the football field was densely planted with vine maples, aspens, pines, and scrub roses, providing for a colorful display of reds, oranges, and yellows mixed among the green from the pines. I'd sat back to enjoy the beauty of the hillside, which was why I happened to see the brief flash of light as the sun reflected off something hidden among the trees. I narrowed my gaze and focused on the spot where I'd seen the flash. If I were a stalker intent on taking photos of Chelsea as she led the cheers for the game, setting up camp in the shelter of the dense woods would be a perfect location, if I happened to have a telephoto lens and didn't need to get close to the action.

"Whatcha looking at?" Mac asked after she handed me my soda, moved my jacket, and sat down beside me.

"I saw a flash of light over there on the hill. I thought it might have been the sun reflecting off something."

"Like a camera?"

"Exactly like a camera. The problem is, with all the trees I can't really see anything, and by the time I walk all the way over there and climb the hill the photographer, if that's what I saw, will have seen me coming and be long gone. I wish I had binoculars."

"Maybe someone brought some. I've seen spectators with them from time to time. Let's keep an eye out."

I continued to stare at the spot where I'd seen the flash. On one hand, the hill was the perfect place from which to gather shots unnoticed; on the other, once the sun went down the photographer would need to use a flash, which I would think would give away their location. I suppose the photographer could have special film or a lens that would allow them to take photos in the dark. I didn't know all that much about photography. I realized it was equally as likely that the flash I'd seen had just been a reflection off a piece of metal on the ground, or even a discarded soda can. I knew I wasn't going to be able to figure this out without getting up and traipsing across the field and up the hill, so I decided to relax and enjoy the game. I turned and looked back to Mac. "How's your corn dog?"

"Really good. Want a bite?"

I shook my head. "No, thanks. I'm saving room for dinner. I'm sure Trevor will want to go to Pirates Pizza and I always overeat when I go there."

"I bet a lot of the team will show up there. I hope it won't be too crowded; we did promise Caleb we'd check out the house tonight."

"Caleb said he'd be there until nine or ten, so I'm sure any pranksters, human or otherwise, won't show up until after that."

"I'm kind of surprised Caleb didn't take a night off to come to the game," Mac said. "He's usually a big supporter."

"This is his last Haunted Hayride at Seacliff High. I think it's important to him to go out with a bang after four years of working on the event. He's spending all his free time at the house, which I guess I understand. There's a lot still to do and Halloween is only a little more than a week away. I'm sure he'll come to the home games in November and the championship series, if we make it that far."

"We will."

"Oh look, here come the cheerleaders." My eyes returned to the hillside where I'd seen the flash of light despite my decision to relax and enjoy the game, but the sun had moved and I wasn't sure whether even if there was a photographer on the hillside the sun would create a reflection. "Any luck tracking down the burner cell?"

"Not yet. I was pretty busy at the office today and didn't have time to work on it. As for the school staff members who have access to the list of student passwords, there are only three: the principal, the computer lab teacher, and the school's IT guy."

"That's it? Just three?"

"That's it in an official capacity, but we both know the principal's access may extend to his secretary, if he needed help with monitoring, and the computer teacher's to subs. The fact that each student creates their own password provides an illusion of privacy, but the fact is, enough people have access to those passcodes that anything sent or received via those accounts should be considered open to public scrutiny. I think we'll need something more specific to go on if we want to track the hacks to a specific person."

"What about the times the photos were sent?" I asked. "Were they all sent during school hours or were some sent on weekends or after-hours?"

Mac frowned. "I didn't look at that. I will. I guess if some of the photos were sent from a computer housed at the school after hours it might narrow down the suspect pool. Other than the janitor and the principal, I'm not sure who might have a key to the building, but I guess we could find out."

"Do teachers have keys?" I asked.

"I don't think so, but I don't know it for a fact. I'll look in to it on Monday, if we haven't wrapped this up by then. Oh look, here come the guys."

Mac and I both stood up and chanted Trevor's name. He looked pretty fine in his uniform. Sometimes I had a hard time reconciling my goofball friend, who was overly fond of his own dumb jokes, with the man on the field, who not only took charge of this team but the game as he led the Pirates to one victory after another.

In the end, the Pirates won by a touchdown in the final minutes. Trevor was on top of the world and everyone wanted to congratulate him, so by the time we left Pirates Pizza and made our way to the house we believed might be haunted it was well after ten.

Chapter 4

"I hope we didn't miss the show," Mac said as we chose a room to use as home base.

"I didn't notice any new graffiti or vandalized props, so if the human intruders plan to show up they haven't yet arrived. As for the living-impaired visitors, should there be any, I have the feeling it's early yet."

"Did we bring snacks?" Trevor asked.

"You ate almost an entire large pizza yourself," I pointed out.

"I know, but I'm a growing boy. If you want me to be alert for spook patrol I'm going to need snacks."

"I brought an entire backpack full of your favorites," Mac said.

Trevor smiled and dug into the bag, coming up with cookies and a cola. I'd known Mac and Trevor for over a year now, and in that time neither had said anything that would lead me to believe they were more than friends. In fact, both had been involved in other relationships. Still, Mac seemed to anticipate Trevor's needs to what seemed to me to be an extreme degree, and he seemed to anticipate hers as well. Now, the fact that they seemed to be hypersensitive to each other could simply be the result of a lifelong friendship, but there were times, like now, when I wondered if their feelings ran deeper than either admitted.

"This place kind of gives me the creeps," Mac said after we settled in. "When we were here during daylight it wasn't so bad, but I didn't realize how dark it would be tonight."

"Caleb has portable lights that are powered by a generator; he moves them around with him when he works here at night. I don't think we should use them, though, because we want to attract any nocturnal guests, not scare them away," I said. "The battery-powered lanterns should be fine, but if we need more light for some reason Caleb showed me how to run the generator."

"Okay, so what do we do until the spooks show?" Trevor asked as he dug around in the backpack for more snacks.

"I'm thinking we should do a sweep of the house every sixty minutes unless we hear something and then we can react to the stimulation at that time," I suggested. "The sweeps will only take about ten or fifteen minutes, so we can just hang out in between."

"We can tell ghost stories," Trevor offered.

"Or not," Mac countered. "When do we start?"

"I thought we'd do our sweeps at random intervals. Not that the ghosts will care, but if there are human visitors we don't want to be too predictable. Let's do the first in about ten minutes."

The first sweep didn't turn up anything, but twenty minutes after we completed it we heard movement on the floor below us. We'd decided to set up our base in one of the empty bedrooms on the second floor so we would hear any movement coming from either the first floor or the attic.

"Those are definitely human footsteps," I whispered.

"Should we confront whoever it is?" Mac asked, scooting just a bit closer to Trevor.

"No. We don't have weapons and because we were going to be late, I didn't go all the way home for Tucker. I think we should quietly check it out. We'll stay in the shadows until we know what we're dealing with. We can always call the cops if we need to."

"Maybe we should call the cops now," Mac suggested.

"It's probably just kids," I countered. "It sounds like they're making their way up the stairs. We found footprints in the attic that looked like children's, so they may have supplies hidden up there. Let's separate. Trevor and I will check that out. Mac, you head outside. If we get into trouble you can call for help."

"Okay," Mac agreed. "But I want to go on record as saying I don't like this one little bit."

Trevor and I slowly crept up the stairs with him in the lead. Moving slowly allowed us not to make any noise that would alert the intruders of our presence. I could hear voices in the attic as we neared the top of the stairs, which confirmed in my mind that we were indeed dealing with kids.

Once we arrived I cracked the door open. Sure enough, there were three young boys— around ten, I thought—moving boxes to the side to get to the ones at the bottom. I watched as they opened one and took out cans of spray paint, a big hammer, and a much smaller ax.

"What do you think you're doing?" Trevor demanded as he flung the door fully open.

The kids were obviously startled and immediately fell into a defensive position. I could see they wanted to run, but Trevor was blocking the only door.

I moved around Trevor's massive body and stepped inside the room. "It looks like we've found our vandals."

"We're not vandals," one of the boys, the tallest and thinnest, argued.

"According to my friend Caleb, he's found damaged props and graffiti on the walls the past few days. Based on the things in your hands, I'd say the three of you have been behind the problems he's been having."

"Maybe we should call the cops and let them sort it out," Trevor said.

"No, please," pleaded a short, chubby boy with blond hair that fell over his eyes. "My parents will kill me."

"You should have thought of that before you damaged property that wasn't yours," Trevor countered.

"But it *is* ours. This house. It *is* ours," the third boy, a redhead with a face full of freckles, claimed.

"The house is yours?" I asked. "You own it?"

The redhead glanced at his tall, skinny friend, who answered. "No, but Mr. Weston said we could have our hangout here. He let us use the whole second floor. I know he's dead, but no one has been in here since, so we figured we were in the clear to keep using it. Then those teenagers showed up and ruined everything. This is our hangout."

"Yeah," the redhead added. "We were here first, and everyone knows possession is nine-tenths of the law."

Trevor chuckled. "You know that for a fact, do you?"

"My big brother says it all the time," the boy insisted.

"Does your brother tend to steal things?" Trevor guessed.

The boy bowed his head and didn't answer.

"Okay, say you're right," I jumped in. "Say you'd been using the house for a long time and then Caleb and his crew showed up and ruined it for you. They'll only be here for another week. It would have been smarter to wait until they were gone rather than destroy things."

"They deserved to have their stuff destroyed," the chubby blond said, a hint of anger in his voice. "We had a lot of good stuff in the big room on the second floor and they took it all away. I heard someone say it ended up in the dump."

"Did Caleb know you'd been using the house for a fort?"

"It's not a fort; it's a hangout," the boy argued.

I glanced at Trevor, who just shrugged. I turned back to the boys. "Did the teenagers who showed up and took your stuff know you'd been using the house as a hangout and the things in that room were yours?"

The tall, thin boy admitted they probably had no idea.

I glanced once again at Trevor, who was still standing in the doorway. "Text Mac and tell her to come on up." I turned back to the boys. "I understand why you're mad that Caleb and the others got rid of your stuff and messed up your clubhouse."

"Hangout," all three boys said in unison.

"Oh, right. But even if they wrecked your hangout you need to understand that they didn't know the stuff was yours. They have permission from Mr. Weston's nephew to use the house for a Haunted Hayride next weekend. After that they'll be done with the place. If I find a way to compensate you for the loss of your belongings will you stop vandalizing the place and allow the high school to use your hangout for another week and a half?"

"What's compensate?" the chubby blond asked.

"It means I'll help you get some stuff to replace what you lost. What did Caleb take to the dump?"

"A perfectly good couch we found on the curb, a couple of tables my mom was getting rid of, a big chest Mr. Weston gave us that we used to hide our treasures, a two-way radio; all sorts of stuff," the tall kid answered.

"I'll take you to the secondhand store when the Haunted Hayride is over and you can pick out some new stuff if you agree to leave things alone until Caleb is done with the house."

"What if we don't agree?" the redhead asked.

"Then I'll have no choice but to call the police."

The three boys huddled together to discuss the situation. After a bit they turned around.

"Okay," the tall, skinny kid said. "We'll let them use our hangout for their hayride if you replace our stuff and let us keep that big skeleton by the front door."

I stuck out my hand. "Deal."

The boys looked at one another. Finally, the redhead asked if they could leave.

"Before you do, I have to ask how you've been getting in and out. The house is locked up tight every night."

"There's a secret passage that starts off in the forest and ends up in the basement," the redhead said.

"Can you show me where it is?"

"You asking to take our tour?" the boy asked.

I smiled. "Sure, I'd love to take the tour."

"That'll be ten bucks," he informed me.

"Okay. I have money in my backpack downstairs. If you follow us I'll get it."

The tall, thin kid looked toward the door, where Trevor was still waiting, and Mac had just joined him. "That's ten bucks each," he added.

******

The doorway in the cellar was hidden behind a large wooden cabinet that had been pulled out from the wall. The passage itself was dark and narrow, but the boys had flashlights and Trevor, Mac, and I had grabbed our own as well. The passage had a damp feel to it and I wondered if groundwater seeped through when it rained. I could hear the echo of waves crashing in the distance, so I suspected the passage opened up even closer to the water than the house.

No one spoke as we walked in single file. About halfway along the passage we came to a fork, with a second passage heading off in another direction.

"What does that lead to?" I stopped walking, causing Mac and Trevor, who were behind me, to stop as well.

"Another door," the redhead answered. "But it's locked."

"Have you ever tried to open it?" I wondered.

All three said they hadn't.

"Mr. Weston said not to ever go down that passage and especially not to touch the door," the dark-haired boy explained. "It was one of the rules he gave us when he agreed to let us use the second floor as a hangout. We did sneak down there once, and we touched the door, but then we all had pains in our hearts. We were curious, but Mr. Weston was a nice man who was doing a nice thing for us, so we never tried to open it."

"Did he ever say what was on the other side of the door?" Mac asked.

"No," the blond answered. "He didn't, but I think it must be something with magical powers. Maybe something like an evil spirit or a dimension monster. Can't think of no other reason touching a door would make you hurt inside."

I turned and looked at Mac and Trevor. I could see the question on their faces but didn't comment further. "Okay. Thanks for the information. How far to the end?"

"Not too far," the tall, thin kid answered. "Stay real close. The passage gets steep at the end, so you have to walk real slow, but it isn't too bad because it hasn't rained for a while."

"It's bad when it rains?"

The boy nodded. "When it rains the water runs down and you can't get through that way."

"Have you ever been trapped in here?" I asked.

"No," the redhead answered. "If it's raining we just use the front door."

Once we'd made our way out of the tunnel and into the forest, which couldn't be more than a hundred yards from the sea, I gave the boys my cell number and asked them to call me the day after Halloween. I figured Caleb would have his stuff cleared out by then and I would take the boys shopping to replace the things they'd lost. I reminded them that part of the deal was their cooperation and they all agreed to stay away from the house until after Caleb and the volunteers had cleared out.

"You realize they could say they lost anything," Mac said as we started back through the tunnel to the house. "This may end up being a very expensive shopping trip."

"I know, but I can afford to buy them some things and I do feel bad their stuff was hauled away. I bet Caleb will too when he finds out what happened."

"Yeah, you're probably right," Mac agreed. "I won't be a bit surprised, though, if the boys tell you they had the newest gaming system hidden in that room."

I shrugged. I didn't care. As it turned out, the boys had given us some valuable information I wasn't quite sure what to do with. I paused when we came to the fork in the passage and made a quick decision, heading down the other route to the secret room.

"Are you planning to open the door?" Trevor asked. "Because I've been dying to ever since the kids mentioned it."

"Maybe," I answered. "I definitely intend to check it out."

As the boys had described, there was a sturdy door with a heavy lock at the end of the second passage. We didn't have anything with us that would open the door, but the minute I put my hand on it I sensed a deep longing that tore at my soul. I gasped as fear and sadness gripped my heart so deeply that it created a physical pain.

"What is it?" Mac asked.

I lowered my hand and took a step back. "I'm not sure, but I know we need to open this door. Whatever's on the other side seems to be the source of a deep sorrow, just like the boys suggested. I'm not sure I've ever felt such a strong presence. The lock is sturdy, but I'm sure we have something in our tool kit back at home that will cut it."

"You want to go now?" Trevor asked.

I felt my breath catch as I considered the depth of the pain I'd just experienced. "I have to go now. I'll grab Shadow while I'm there. He seems to have a sense about these things."

Chapter 5

Mom was out when Trevor, Mac, and I arrived at my house, but both Tucker and Shadow were happy to see us. I texted my mom to tell her what we were doing before going out to the shed to see what I could find that would handle the lock on the door. I selected a large bolt cutter, as well as a prying tool, a screwdriver, and a hammer. I wasn't sure we'd need all that, but it made sense to be prepared.

I put the tools in the Jeep, then went back for Shadow and Tucker. I wasn't sure we needed Tucker, but there was no way I was taking Shadow and leaving him home. I grabbed a couple of extra flashlights just in case we needed them, and then the three of us, along with Tucker and Shadow, returned to the haunted house.

Upon arriving, we immediately went down into the basement, through the doorway, and into the passage. When we came to the locked door Trevor used the bolt cutters. The door was heavy, so it took all three of us to work it open. Inside, we used our flashlights to illuminate the small room. There were two wooden boxes, handmade, one large and one small, both nailed shut and both shaped suspiciously like coffins.

"Are you sure we should open them?" Trevor asked.

"I'm sure," I said.

"What if there are vampires inside?" Trevor added, taking a step back.

"There are no such things as vampires," I informed him.

"This coming from the girl who sees ghosts?"

I grabbed the hammer Mac was holding and began to pry at the nails. "Ghosts and vampires are completely different things. Now grab that screwdriver and help me pry the lid open once I loosen the nails."

It took a few minutes, but eventually, I opened the first box. I gasped when I realized I was looking at the skeleton of a child. I could feel fear and grief overtake me as I stood looking down at the remains, but I hadn't seen the ghost I was expecting to find.

"It's just a kid," Mac said softly.

"Yeah." I let out a long breath. I glanced at Trevor, who had turned pale. "Help me get the lid off the other box."

The second box also contained the remains of a person, this one an adult.

"So who are they?" Trevor asked.

"I have no idea," I said.

"Can you see them?" Mac asked. "I mean the ghosts of them, of course."

I shook my head. "No. But I can feel them. I sense pain and sorrow but also fear. And there's something else."

"Like what?" Mac asked.

"I'm not sure exactly." I shone my light around the room, which was empty except for a cabinet that was pushed against the back wall. "I really want to look around, but I think we should call the police. Maybe if they can find out who the skeletons belong to we can find out why they're here."

I walked over to the cabinet and opened the door. Inside were blankets, clothing, toys, and books. It looked like these were things that could have belonged to both skeletons.

"This is just too disturbing," Mac said.

"Yeah." I sighed. "It really is." I paused. "Do you feel a draft?"

Mac stopped, then shook her head.

"Maybe you feel the fresh air coming into the room from the passageway," Trevor suggested.

"I suppose." I continued to look around the room but didn't see a source other than the door where fresh air may have entered.

"I wonder what happened to them," Mac whispered.

"The old man who lived here must have killed them," Trevor stated. "He must have kept them locked down here and then, when he was tired of them, he must have killed them."

Mac looked at me. "Do you think that's what happened?"

"Maybe. It seems like a good theory, but until we figure it out for sure I don't think these two souls will be able to move on. Let's get back upstairs and call this in."

"We should let Caleb know what's going on," Mac added.

"Yeah. I'll call him after I call the cops."

Mac, Trevor, and I discussed what to tell the police and what to keep to ourselves. We all agreed we didn't want to get the three kids in trouble for breaking into the house, so we decided we'd say we were checking on the props that had been left in the house and had discovered the passage when we were looking around. Then, during our exploration of the passage, we'd found the room. We called Caleb and told him the same thing. He was coming to meet us at the house as soon as he could get there.

A short time later, two police officers arrived. One, a veteran officer named Dick Wharton, complained that he was less than two weeks from retirement and didn't need such a complicated case so late in his career, and the other, a brand-new officer named Woody Baker, who'd joined the force after completing a two-year tour of duty with the Marines. While Officer Wharton was irritated to be bothered with the mystery, Officer Baker was eager to dig in and get his hands dirty. I wondered how these very different men had ended up as partners. Maybe the older man had been assigned to break in the younger one, who barely looked old enough to have been in the armed forces before becoming a cop, but from Baker's eager grin and genuine enthusiasm, I was willing to bet he was driving Wharton crazy with all his questions.

"The medical examiner is on his way," Wharton informed us. "I need to take a statement from each of you. I prefer to do the interviews individually. Officer Baker will escort Ms. Reynolds and Mr. Johnson to the main floor of the house while I speak to Ms. Prescott. We'll use one of the rooms on the second floor for our interviews."

I offered Mac and Trevor encouraging smiles. "That's fine," I said to Wharton. "I'm happy to tell you everything I know, which, I'll warn you, isn't a lot."

I followed the officer up the stairs. There was a long table along one wall that Caleb had been using to draw diagrams of the setup for the props. There weren't any chairs, so I pulled over a sturdy box and sat on it. Wharton did the same.

"Please state your full name and address," he said after taking a small notepad and pen out of his shirt pocket.

"Alyson Prescott," I said, following up with my address. My heart was pounding. So far, I hadn't had to subject my new identity to police scrutiny. I hadn't had a problem using my new ID to register for school or to get a driver's license, but I was afraid the police might take a closer look at what was in reality an illusion.

"Why exactly were you in this house this evening?" Wharton asked.

"My friend, Caleb Wellington, is in charge of the Haunted Hayride the high school puts on every year as a fund-raiser. We agreed to stop by to check on the house, and while we were here we took a look around. During our exploration of the house we found the secret room. When we realized what was inside we called you."

"Do you have contact information for Mr. Wellington?"

"I do, but we called him right after we called you. He should be here shortly."

"Has anyone else other than the three of you been on the property this evening?"

"Caleb and a handful of volunteers were here earlier, but they left by ten." I figured not mentioning the three boys wasn't really lying; the worst I could be accused of was selective truth telling.

"It appeared the lock on the door to the room where the skeletons were found had been tampered with."

I nodded. "The room was locked when we found it. I think it must have been locked for a long time. I guess our curiosity got the better of us and we used tools I had in my Jeep to break into the room. The previous owner of the house is dead and his nephew said it was okay with him if we used any part of the property we found useful."

Wharton frowned as he jotted down a few notes. I hoped the fact that I'd just admitted to breaking into the locked room wasn't going to get us into trouble.

"Did you know the previous resident of the house?" Wharton asked.

"No. The man who lived here was named Eliston Weston. He died two years ago and I just moved to Cutter's Cove a little over a year ago."

"I see. Where did you live before?"

My mind went blank and I scrambled for the answer. "Minnesota," I said, finally remembering my cover. "I have to say, the weather in Oregon is a lot nicer."

"Yes, I imagine it is. Do you have any idea who the skeletons you discovered might belong to?"

I shook my head. "I'm afraid not. It looks as if they were there for a long time. I've been told Mr. Weston lived in the house for thirty years. Unless the remains turn out to be older than that, I assume he was the one to put them there."

Wharton asked me a few more questions and then escorted me back into the room where Baker was waiting with Mac and Trevor. Wharton asked Mac to follow him into the room upstairs. I nodded at her to let her know I'd stuck to our story as we passed on my way in and her way out.

Caleb showed up while Mac was being interviewed. I introduced him to Officer Baker, who, I realized, was pretty darn good-looking for a cop. During our conversation, I learned he was just twenty-one and had attended Seacliff High, although being four years ahead of Mac and Trevor, they'd never attended the school at the same time. After we chatted a bit I realized we had quite a few friends and acquaintances in common.

"I'm sorry we went snooping," I whispered to Caleb while Trevor was talking football with Baker. "I know this puts you in a tough spot. I really hope they won't force you to cancel the Hayride."

"With two skeletons on the property, I'm sure they will. Even if the police release the house in a few days we probably won't have time to set things up."

"Whoever was left in that room had been dead for a long time. I can't believe there'd be a lot of clues to find all these years later, so maybe they won't need to secure the house for long."

Caleb didn't look convinced. "I wonder who the skeletons belong to."

I shrugged. "The only thing I can tell you is that one of them was a child."

"And the other one?"

"An adult. Based on the height, I'd guess a man. Both bodies were completely decomposed, but the wooden boxes they placed in weren't exactly air tight, and it looked as if moisture got in as well."

"The previous owner had lived in the house for three decades. It seems like he must either have been the killer or he was protecting the killer."

"Most likely. Here comes Mac. If they speak to you don't bring up the vandalism. I'll fill you in later."

Trevor went with Wharton next and Mac joined Caleb and me. Baker stayed with us.

"Look," he said, I assumed to calm Mac down after her interview, "I know things like this can be pretty nerve-racking, but it's best to just relax and tell us what you know. It's obvious the skeletons were in that room since before any of us were born. You aren't suspects, just witnesses."

"We know that," Mac answered as she bent down to pet Tucker, who had approached her when she returned to the room. Tucker was very sensitive and always seemed to sense when someone needed comforting. "But it's still pretty upsetting to be interrogated by a man who's totally devoid of facial expression."

Baker chuckled. "Yeah, that's Wharton for you. Mr. Stoic. But he's a fair man who just wants to put in his time, so I doubt you'll hear from him after tonight. I, on the other hand, plan to be very involved in this case. A couple of the other cops are out on medical leave, so I may be able to work my way into this investigation." Baker glanced at a spot behind where I was standing. "What's that cat doing?"

I turned around and saw a boy peeking out from behind the old red drapes that covered the window. Shadow was batting at his leg. I knew instinctively that the child I saw was the spirit of the boy who'd been in the room. He looked scared and unsure, as confused as I was about what was going on. I smiled at him but didn't bring his presence to anyone else's attention. I wasn't sure when I'd be able to come back to the house. The police would probably wrap the whole place up in yellow tape once we left, I had an odd feeling the boy was frightened by the other spirit that had been set free, but I couldn't be certain.

The boy bent down and put his arms around Shadow. It almost looked as if an exchange of energy had occurred between them. The cat began to purr and the boy, who might be eight or nine, smiled. Shadow had helped calm my fears on more than one occasion; I hoped the boy was finding peace in his presence.

Mac was staring at me with a strange expression on her face. I knew she couldn't see the boy and figured she was wondering what I was staring at. I tilted my head just a bit and she noticed Shadow's tail, which was clearly evident from behind the drape, where he must have followed the child. I could no longer see the boy, but I sensed he was still in the room.

"Are you okay, miss?" Baker asked with an expression of genuine concern on his face.

"I'm fine. I'm just wondering what my cat is up to." I nodded toward the drape.

Baker laughed. "It looks like he's hiding from us. I take it he isn't a big fan of the local police."

"Shadow is new to Cutter's Cove and I'm not sure how he feels about men in blue. He probably just found a mouse. Is it okay if I go over to check on him?"

"Sure. Go ahead."

I thanked the officer and walked to the curtain. I separated it in the middle and took a step behind it, then said aloud, "Shadow, what are you up to?" Then I whispered to the boy, "Don't be scared. I'm here to help you."

The boy faded away, though I could feel him still there.

"I'll come back tomorrow night. Meet me in the tunnel. I'll bring Shadow."

The cat meowed and the boy reappeared.

"I have to go now," I said, picking up the cat. The boy faded away again and I went back to the other side of the room, where Officer Baker was chatting with Trevor and Mac. "Did Caleb go in for an interview?" I asked.

"Yeah, just a minute ago," Trevor said. "Is Shadow okay?"

"Yeah. He found something behind the curtain." I looked at Baker. "Will you need us to stay once Caleb's been interviewed?"

"I'll need to check with Officer Wharton, but I doubt it."

"And the Hayride?" I asked. "Will we be able to have it as planned?"

"I'm not sure," Baker said. "It isn't up to me, but it would be a shame to cancel it. I went on the Hayride when I went to Seacliff High and it was always an awesome event. If you call me tomorrow I should have a better idea of how things are going to play out."

Officer Baker took a business card out of his pocket and jotted a number on the back. "The number on the back is my cell number. Feel free to call me on that line if you can't get through by calling the precinct. If I can help smooth the way for the Hayride I will."

I smiled as I accepted the card.

Shortly afterward Caleb returned to the room along with Officer Wharton, who counseled us to refrain from discussing with other people what we'd found until they'd had the chance to complete their investigation. He also said he'd likely be in touch with additional questions when they'd had a chance to figure out what it was they were dealing with.

"Will they take the skeletons to the morgue?" I asked Baker after Wharton headed back to the basement and the passage to the secret room.

"The ME is on the way. It would seem there might not be a lot to learn from remains that are little more than bones, but you'd be surprised."

"Will you let us know what the medical examiner finds out?"

Baker looked uncertain. "I won't be able to share information relating to an open case, but once the case is closed I don't see why I can't share our findings with you."

"Thank you." I smiled again. "I have to admit to being curious."

As we turned to leave I caught a glimpse of a man at the top of the stairs. Like the boy, he was a very well-formed ghost, tall, with dark hair and old clothing. His hair was long and he had a wild look about him that sent a shiver down my spine. One of his hands was clutched in a fist that he raised when he realized I could see him. I felt an iciness touch my soul as he looked right through me. Suddenly, I was worried about the boy. Of course he was dead and I wasn't sure you could physically hurt someone who was already dead, but I had to assume based on my previous experience with ghosts that they retained memories and feelings. I knew the boy was afraid of the man, but given the fact that I was being escorted out of the house by a policeman, there wasn't a lot I could do other than pray that I'd be able to get back here soon, and that when I did return, I'd be able to help the boy move on to a happier, safer place.

Chapter 6

Saturday, October 21

Trevor, Mac, and I planned to return to the house via the hidden passage at around ten o'clock that night. We hoped to make a connection with the ghost of the child in the hope of learning more about him so that we could help him move on. The house had been taped off, but when I'd checked earlier in the day I'd seen that the entrance to the passage the three boys had shown us was still wide open. We'd park on the street and then walk through the dense forest to the opening so as not to attract attention.

It was just ten days until Halloween and I'd yet to buy any pumpkins, so I talked both Mac and Trevor into joining me at the pumpkin patch on Dooley's Farm, a magical place in the Oregon hills. It sat overlooking the ocean, with hundreds of Christmas trees of various heights covering the hillside. In the flat meadow at the base of the trees, hundreds of pumpkins grew on bright green vines. There was a large red barn with rows of picnic tables off to the left. Behind the barn was a large pond where children were fishing, their parents snapping pictures.

"How many pumpkins are we looking for?" Trevor asked as he grabbed one of the green wagons the farm provided to haul the pumpkins you chose.

"I guess maybe six large ones and two or three small ones. I want two big ones for carving and four for the front porch, and I thought I'd make a centerpiece for the table with small pumpkins and fall leaves."

Mac looked off into the distance, where the hillside was painted in red, orange, and yellow. "Do you need to gather leaves as well?"

"We have quite a few colorful trees on our property, but a hike in the hills would be perfect on a day like this."

"While hiking sounds like fun, I really want to head to the costume shop after this," Trevor said. "If we don't get our costumes for the Hayride today everything will be picked over."

"Do you think there'll even be a hayride?" Mac asked.

"Hard to tell," I answered as we started down the path to the pumpkin patch. "If it's canceled we can put together a party for our friends. Either way, we'll need costumes."

"Something gory," Trevor insisted.

"I think I'll be a zombie in honor of my new game," Mac commented.

"Okay, gory it is," I agreed. "Oh, look at this one over here." I jogged over to a huge pumpkin that would most likely take all three of us to lift. "It would look perfect next to the front door."

"We'll need another wagon," Mac said.

"I'll go grab one after we get this one loaded," Trevor offered. "We can leave the first one near the checkout counter. I'm sure they'll hang on to it for us until we pick out the rest."

Mac and I continued to examine pumpkins, looking for ones with perfect shapes, after Trevor left to get the second wagon.

"Isn't that Officer Baker over near the corn maze?" Mac asked.

"It sure looks like him. I guess he must be off duty today."

"It looks like he's with those two little boys."

"Should we go over to say hi?"

Mac looked at me and then back at Officer Baker. "I think it would be the polite thing to do."

"Maybe he has something he can tell us."

"I guess it wouldn't hurt to ask. Even if he can't say much he might let something slip, or we may be able to figure out what's going on from his body language or what he intentionally doesn't say."

Mac and I set aside the pumpkins we were looking at and headed in the direction of the corn maze. When we got close to where Officer Baker was standing, we both said hello.

"Ms. Prescott; Ms. Reynolds," he greeted us.

"You can call me Alyson."

"And I'm Mac."

"Okay, then, hello, Alyson and Mac. I'm Woody. Are you here to do the maze?"

"Looking for pumpkins," I explained. "Are these your sons?" I asked, gesturing to the two boys, who both looked about three.

"My sister's kids. Jimmy and Johnny, meet Alyson and Mac."

The boys hid behind their uncle.

"Sorry about that. The boys aren't real comfortable around strangers."

"Not a problem," I said. "Some kids that age are shy by nature. We don't want to take up any of your time on your day off; we just saw you standing here and wanted to thank you for last night. Your calmness offset the iciness of your partner."

"Wharton is okay once you get to know him."

Mac spotted Trevor coming back up the hill and waved to him to let him know we'd changed our location.

"I don't suppose you've heard anything about the fate of the Hayride?" I asked.

"The crime scene guys are at the house today, but I understand they plan to be done there by the end of the day. Their decision to release the house or keep it taped off will depend on what they find. The reality is, there most likely won't be much to find. The victims died a long time ago and a lot of people will have been in the house since then."

"Have you identified the two skeletons?" I asked.

Woody shook his head. "I ran missing persons reports for male children and adult males reported missing from the area between fifteen and thirty years ago, but so far I haven't found anything. It will help if the ME can nail down a tighter timeline, but our little department doesn't have the equipment it would take to determine time of death so long ago. We'll need to send the remains out if we can't determine identity, cause, and time of death another way."

"If you wouldn't be endangering the investigation in any way, will you let us know if you find out who the skeletons were?" I asked.

"I can do that, as long as it won't hinder the investigation."

Trevor joined us, so Mac and I said our good-byes and headed back to the pumpkin patch.

"What was that all about?" Trevor asked.

"Just trying to get intel on the two skeletons. So far, the cops don't seem to know anything. Woody said he'd let us know if they do."

"Woody?" Trevor asked.

"He told us to call him Woody," I said. "I saw a couple more pumpkins I want over by the eastern border. Let's head over there first; then we can continue up the hill."

******

By the time we got to the costume shop it was packed. I guess we should have realized the Saturday before Halloween weekend would be a busy one for a store that sold costumes and decorations. Trevor seemed frustrated by the crowd, but I was enjoying spending the day in a town all decked out for the holiday, with window decorations and orange twinkle lights in all the trees lining Main.

"I'm going to need face paint," Mac said right off the bat. "A lot of it."

"What do you plan to wear?" I asked.

"I'm just going to rip up some old clothes and cover them in fake blood. Getting the face paint just right will be the tricky part."

"How about you?" I asked Trevor. "Are you going the face paint or the scary mask route?"

"Mask. That way I can just take if off if I get some lip action on the night of the party."

"Lip action?" I laughed. "You're such a nerd."

"Not just a nerd but king of the nerds."

I rolled my eyes as Trevor picked up a disgusting mask and pulled it over his head.

"How about you?" Mac asked. "Are you going to get a mask?"

"I think I'm just going to make a costume from things I have at home. I need to pick up a few things for my mom, so how about I meet you back at the car in half an hour?"

Trevor and Mac both looked at me with suspicion on their faces, but eventually she noticed my look of desperation. "Yeah, okay," she said, taking Trevor by the arm.

I left the costume shop and hurried down the block to Chan's Occult Shop. I'd been wanting to talk to him about my dream, but he'd been out of town, so I hadn't had the chance. When we'd driven by on our way to the costume shop I'd noticed an "Open" sign on the door.

The bell on top of the door jingled as I walked in. The store was quite large inside. One wall was completely covered with shelves of books that reached to the ceiling. There was a counter to the right with a cash register and a glass case that held the more valuable items. The center of the store was lined with shelves bearing glass jars filled with all sorts of strange-looking things.

"Chan," I called, when he didn't immediately appear. "Are you here?"

The small man with his perpetual smile poked his head over the half railing lining the loft on the second floor. "Amanda. How nice to see you."

"I hoped you'd have a few minutes to chat. Can I come up?"

"Certainly. You know my door is always open to you."

I climbed the stairs to the second story, which was stocked with jars filled with newt eyes and chicken feet as well as different-colored crystals and powders that weren't labeled, though I assumed Chan knew the identity of. I still remembered being completely freaked out the first time I'd visited his shop and even more freaked out when he'd called me Amanda. Since that first meeting, however, I'd come to know and respect him. More importantly, I trusted him.

"You've been having dreams," Chan jumped right in.

"Yes. How did you know?"

Chan placed a hand on mine. "As I have said in the past, I've been charting your essence."

"So what does it mean? Am I in danger?"

Chan led me into a back room and instructed me to sit down. He poured me a cup of tea from a pot that had been sitting on his desk. He took a sip of his own tea and waited for me to follow before he answered.

"I sense the focal point in your dream is a door."

"It is. A dark door at the top of several steps."

"I suspect the door in your dream represents a barrier between what you know and what you want and need to know. It may have a physical form or not. My sense is that the purpose of the dream is to bring you closer to the place you need to be to resolve your conflict. Once you can overcome your fears and accept what it is your mind wants you to know, you will have the answers you seek."

"So the door I need to find and open may not be real?"

"That is unclear to me at this time. While it is true you may one day stumble onto the door in your dreams, it is equally likely you won't."

"So what do I do? How do I get rid of the dream?"

"Tell me exactly what you see and feel."

"I'm alone and it's dark. There's an old house with several steps leading up to a dark-colored door. I instinctively know that my destiny resides on the other side of the door, but I'm terrified to open it. When I first had the dream I'd wake up in a cold sweat after placing one foot on the first step, but over time I've been able to maintain my dream state longer. I'm now able to climb the stairs and open the door. The moment I step inside, though, I'm filled with overwhelming terror. I scream and wake up."

"And you do not have a sense of what you see once you open the door?" Chan asked as he topped off my teacup.

I shook my head. "I can only see a white light that's blinding me, but I feel both terror and hopelessness. I haven't been able to sleep in months. It's gotten to the point where I'm falling asleep in class. You need to help me conquer this."

"The dream is yours to conquer."

"Can it hurt me?"

"That depends on you. You can let the dream destroy you or you can take charge of the images in your mind and make them show you what it is you need to know."

"But do you sense I'm in danger? Actual danger, not dream danger?"

Chan paused before he answered. He took my hand in his and closed his eyes. It almost seemed like he'd dozed off, but after several minutes he opened his eyes.

"So?" I asked.

"There is a darkness surrounding you. My sense is that the time of reckoning is near."

"Reckoning?"

"Your aura is fragmented, as is your life. There will come a point when you must choose. It won't be today, but soon."

I felt my throat tighten. "Choose what?"

"Life."

I could feel the blood drain from my face. I'd come to Chan hoping he'd make me feel better, but I was more terrified than I'd ever been before.

"When the time comes I will be there for you. Until then, you have a job to do."

I took several deep breaths, followed by several large sips of tea. It did seem to have a calming effect. I wondered what was in it.

"A job? You mean the bodies in the secret room? Do you know who they are?"

Chan handed me a piece of paper. On it were two names and a single date: *Julius and Bobby, April 12, 1992.*

"Are these the names of the spirits?"

Chan just smiled.

"Do you have last names?"

"You have all you need. Let your heart lead you where you are destined to go."

I hated it when Chan's help wasn't really all that helpful, but things had all worked out in the past, so I decided to go with this. "Okay; thanks." I put the note in my pocket. "I guess I should get going. Mac and Trevor are waiting for me. If you do get any more insight will you let me know? One of the ghosts in the house is a child. I feel he's afraid of the other one. I'd really like to help him move on." I paused and considered the situation. "I'd really like to help them both move on."

"Trust what you know, my young friend."

By the time I returned to my car, Mac and Trevor were both waiting. Trevor immediately picked up on the fact that although I'd told them I needed to pick up some things for my mother, I wasn't carrying a single bag. I made something up about my mom texting at the last minute to let me know she'd bought them herself and then slid into the driver's seat of my Jeep and headed toward home.

Chapter 7

Now that we had names and a date to use as a frame of reference, Mac and I got to work, looking for news articles, missing persons reports, obituaries, anything we could think of that might relate to Julius or Bobby and the date April 12, 1992. Trevor had gone home after getting a call from his mother that some out-of-state relatives had arrived, but he promised to join us when we went back to the house that evening.

"It's going to be hard to find information that might be relevant with only first names," Mac murmured.

"Yeah, I know, but Chan said I had all I needed. Julius is somewhat of an uncommon name. Let's start by running it coupled with the date in the newspaper archives and see what we come up with. Woody said they hadn't found any missing persons, but they didn't have a frame of reference. I wonder if I should call him and give him these names and the date."

"And where are you going to tell him you got them?" Mac asked.

"An anonymous tip?"

Mac rolled her eyes. "All that's going to do is make him suspicious. We need more. Something concrete before we start sharing what we have with the police."

"Normally, I would never even consider sharing clues Chan gave me with the police, but Woody seems different. I think he might actually help us."

Mac stopped what she was doing and sat back in her chair. She gave me a hard look. "Are you crushing on the cute young officer?"

"What?" I protested. "Of course not. I have enough going on in my life that I don't need to be crushing on anyone. I just thought maybe he could help."

Mac continued to stare at me.

"I'm not crushing," I insisted.

"He is pretty cute," Mac admitted.

"And so nice. Did you notice how nice he is?"

"He was nice. He's also an adult and you're in high school."

"I'm not saying I want to date him; I just said he was nice. Besides, I'll be eighteen in two months and he's only four years older than me. If I wanted to date him—and I'm not saying I do—it wouldn't be weird at all."

Mac returned to her computer without responding. She seemed to be focused on what she was doing, but I was certain she was still wondering if I'd lost my mind. I knew I couldn't get involved with anyone right now, especially not a cop, but it had been a long time since I'd even noticed a person of the opposite sex. It felt good to look, even if I could never touch.

After more than an hour of trying to find a link to the date and names Chan had given me we decided to change direction and see what we could find out about Eliston Weston, the previous owner of the house. We knew he'd died two years ago. We also knew he'd purchased the property from Joe and Jenny Jenkins around thirty years before that, which would have been around 1985. Joe and Jenny had owned the house from 1962 to 1985.

"I wonder if we can get the exact date the property changed hands," I said.

"I'm sure we can. I can look at the county records. It might take me a few minutes, though."

"I'll run down to the kitchen and get us a snack," I offered. "We never did have lunch."

Tucker and I went downstairs while Shadow and Mac stayed up in my room to work. Ever since I'd seen Chan that morning I'd found myself looking over my shoulder and jumping at every little sound. My mom was in Portland today for an art show, so it was just Mac and me in the house. I jumped when I thought I felt a presence behind me, but when I turned around there was no one there. I glanced at Tucker, who looked unconcerned, and realized I must be losing my mind. This was no way to live. I needed to get a grip.

I stood in front of the open refrigerator for what seemed like a long time before I decided to make turkey sandwiches and dice up some fruit. Mom had made pumpkin muffins for breakfast the day before, so I added a couple of them to the tray, and a couple of colas as well.

I was about to head back upstairs when my phone rang. I set the tray down and looked at the caller ID. It was a local number I didn't recognize.

"Hello?" I said with a question in my voice.

"Alyson, it's Woody Baker."

"Woody." I smiled. "Do you have news?"

"More like a question. The crime scene guys found fingerprints that haven't been identified but seem to belong to children. The prints were left recently. Do you know if there have been children in the house?"

I let out a sigh before I answered. "There *were* children in the house. Three boys, around ten. I didn't catch their names and I didn't mention them last night because I didn't want them to get into trouble."

"Trouble? Why would they be in trouble?"

"They weren't supposed to be there," I admitted. I decided not to mention the vandalism. "It seems Mr. Weston let the boys have a clubhouse on the second story of the house. No one came to claim the house after he died, so the kids continued to use it. They're nice kids who didn't think they were doing anything wrong. They showed up when we were at the house last night. I explained about the Hayride and they agreed not to enter the house until after the high school was done with it."

"So you spoke to them but didn't ask their names?"

"Yes, that's correct."

"Do you have any reason to believe they knew about the skeletons in the room?"

"I'm certain they didn't."

"Can you describe the boys?"

I paused. "Like I said, I don't want them to get into any trouble. They didn't do anything wrong and they couldn't have known about the skeletons in the boxes, so I don't see any reason to bother them."

"You said they had a clubhouse in Mr. Weston's home. It stands to reason they knew him well. It's also likely the bodies were placed in the coffins during the time Mr. Weston lived in the house. I think we need to know what they might know about Mr. Weston."

I groaned. "You're right. I didn't think of that. I'm so sorry I didn't tell you last night. Your partner was just so intimidating. I was trying to protect the boys from a harsh interrogation."

I waited for Woody to speak. The longer the silence, the more nervous I became. Finally, he spoke. "You said you didn't have the boys' names. Do you have a way to get hold of them?"

I knew all I needed to do was have Mac check school records against their photos; once we had names we could track down addresses.

"Yes, I can get hold of them."

"Okay, how about if you and I speak to them? We'll leave Wharton out of it for now. When we find out what they know we'll decide whether a more formal interview is necessary."

I closed my eyes, trying to decide what to do. "I guess I can live with that. When do you want to meet?"

"This afternoon, if they're available."

"I'll need a couple of hours to track them down. I'll call you after I speak to them."

I hung up, picked up the tray, and continued up the stairs. Mac was looking intently at the computer screen and seemed not to have even noticed my arrival. I set the tray down on the dresser, then turned to look at the screen too. It was a formal document that I supposed contained the ownership history of the Weston house and land.

"I brought food. Did you find something?"

"It looks like the Jenkinses fell behind in their mortgage payments. The bank repossessed the house and put it on the market in February 1985. Mr. Weston paid cash for it in May. The deed was formally transferred from the bank to Mr. Weston on June 3, 1985."

I picked up half of one of the sandwiches and took a bite. "I wonder if any of this means anything."

Mac shrugged. "I'll take a break to eat and then we can keep digging."

"Actually, we need to change direction," I informed Mac. "Woody called. He wants to talk to the boys. It seems their fingerprints are all over the house, although he doesn't have matches for them. He hoped I knew who they were. I told him I didn't, but he says they may know something about Mr. Weston. I guess he has a point. Anyway, he agreed that he and I would speak to them first and leave his scary partner out of it for now. I told him I'd find them and call him back."

"And how are you going to do that?" Mac asked.

"We know what they look like. We suspect they go to the local elementary school and are most likely in fifth or sixth grade. I thought you could hack into the school records to get their names and contact information based on the photos in the student records."

"Of course you did."

"Is that a problem?" I asked.

Mac signed. "No. It's fine. But be careful. Just because the new cop is not only nice but drop-dead gorgeous doesn't mean you can trust him. Be careful what you share with him. I for one don't want to be arrested for hacking into school records."

"I won't tell him where I got the information. I promise."

Mac obtained the names, phone numbers, and addresses for the boys and I tried to decide what to do with the information. If I called the houses chances were one of the parents would answer, and if I just showed up on their doorsteps asking to speak to their sons it was going to look suspicious. I'd pretty much decided to walk down the street where all three boys lived and hoped one of them was outside when it occurred to me that it was Saturday and a lot of the ten-year-olds in town belonged to the youth soccer league. Games were held all day and it was already midafternoon. If the boys did play soccer they would have had an earlier game, but I didn't have anything to lose by looking, so I left Mac working in my room and headed to the soccer field.

There were games on two different fields, so the place was crowded. The first field I checked was occupied by older kids, but on the second one was a game that looked to be fielded with boys of about the right age. At first I didn't see any of the boys I was looking for, but then I spotted the tall, skinny kid running down the field for a goal. I didn't see the other two, but according to the scoreboard there was only two minutes left in the game, so I decided to wait to see if I could find a chance to speak to the kid alone. He must have seen me because as soon as the game was over and the teams broke up, he came over to where I was waiting.

"You change your mind about buying us new stuff?" he asked, a sound of accusation in his voice.

"No. Not at all. But we've hit a snag. After you left my friends and I opened the door in the second passage. We found something that created a situation where we had to call the police. They found your fingerprints in the house and want to talk to you."

"You said no cops."

"I know. I didn't tell them about the vandalism, I promise. I just told them the prints probably belonged to some kids who had a hangout in the house, and they want to talk to you about Mr. Weston. I promise you aren't in trouble. In fact, I got Officer Baker to agree that he and I could speak to all three of you together."

The kid, whose name I now knew was Carlton, looked like he was going to cry.

"Officer Baker is nice. You'll like him. And I'll be there to make sure everything goes smoothly."

"And if we won't talk to him?"

"Then I think the police will come to your home and speak to you anyway. This really is your best bet."

The boy crossed his arms over his chest but didn't answer.

"Look, why don't you talk to Wesley and Alton? If the three of you want to speak to Officer Baker and me instead of whoever shows up from the station call me at the number I gave you. We'll meet wherever the three of you want."

The boy kicked the ground with his toe.

"Please, Carlton. This really will be the easiest on all of you. If I don't hear from you in an hour I'll assume you aren't interested in my offer and I'll call Officer Baker to let him know."

Thankfully, Carlton, Walter, and Alton agreed to meet us at the video arcade at five p.m. I called Woody, who agreed to meet me there. When he showed up in jeans and a sweatshirt rather than his uniform I felt confident I had made a good decision in trusting him.

The video arcade was loud, so Woody suggested we move our conversation outside. There was a small park nearby, so we found an unoccupied bench where we could sit and talk.

"I'm going to ask you some questions and Woody is going to listen in. Is that okay with you?" I asked.

Woody thought it would go better if he was there in an unofficial capacity. The boys all agreed to the plan, so I asked the first of about ten questions Woody and I had prepared. I started by asking the kids to paint a picture of Mr. Weston: how he was as a person and how they all got along together. All the boys seemed to agree he was a nice old man who enjoyed their company. He didn't get out much, but he liked having people in the house, so he'd agreed to let them use the room on the second floor. All three boys seemed to have genuine affection for him and none seemed scared of him, so I was confident the old man's relationship with them was as innocent as it seemed.

The boys also reported that no one else had lived in the house during the year they'd hung out at the house before Mr. Weston died, and they hadn't seen anyone in the house since he'd passed away until

Caleb and the other volunteers. They admitted they knew about the secret passageway but swore they'd never opened the door leading to the room where the skeletons had been found and had no idea what was inside it. When asked if they thought Mr. Weston knew what was in the room, they said they didn't know. He'd just told them never to go in there—which indicated to me that he probably did know.

By the end of the interview Woody and I were both convinced the boys really didn't know anything about the skeletons and that Mr. Weston really had been an old man who both enjoyed the company of kids *and* kept two skeletons in his secret room.

"What do you think?" I asked after the boys went inside to play games with the money I'd given them.

Woody ran his hand through his hair. "I don't know. It seems as if the boys had genuine affection for the old man, but we still need to deal with the elephant in the room."

"The skeletons."

"Exactly."

Chapter 8

Later that evening I returned to the house with Mac, Trevor, and Shadow. We accessed the secret passage via the entrance in the woods so as not to disturb the police tape, which had not yet been removed from the front door. The sky was overcast, blocking the light from the moon, so it was a dark trek through the dense forest.

"Did you hear that?" Mac asked.

I paused. "I think it's just the wind rustling through the trees."

"I'm not talking about that. I'm talking about that screeching sound. At first, I thought it was behind us, but now it seems like it's in front of us."

I stood perfectly still and listened. The wind was blowing hard, creating a quaking sound that seemed to surround us. There *was* a screech, but I was certain it was simply the wind and said so. I began to walk again, slowly, so I wouldn't trip over any of the debris underfoot.

Thunder rolled in from the distance. I was certain we were in for a storm of some significance before the night was over. The cloud cover grew denser, blocking out even the smallest amount of light from the moon. It certainly would have been a lot easier to find our way through the forest with light from above.

"Are you sure this is the right way?" Mac, who was following close behind me, asked as a dog howled in the distance.

"I think so." I tried to create a mental image in my mind of where the access door was in relation to the house when we were there last night.

"Last night it wasn't so dark or windy," Mac pointed out. "Everything seems different."

"And crunchy," Trevor added.

"Crunchy?" I asked.

"I was referring to whatever it is that's crunching under my shoes."

"I've been trying to block that out," Mac admitted.

I set Shadow down on the ground. I'd carried him to this point so I wouldn't lose him in the dark forest, but I assumed the passage was near, so it was time for him to go to work.

"Maybe we should turn back and try again tomorrow," Mac suggested as the first raindrops began to fall.

"It can't be much farther," I answered. "My sense is that Shadow knows where to go, so we'll just follow him. Stay close to one another. We wouldn't want anyone getting lost."

Mac let out a screech when an owl hooted in the distance. The flashlights we'd brought provided a limited amount of light, though not enough to really get a feel for the entire area in which we were walking. The groaning created by the trunks of the trees as they swayed in the wind provided a creepy sort of feeling that, to be honest, we'd be better off without.

"Do you really think the ghosts will show?" Mac asked as we stepped over a large branch that had fallen from a nearby tree.

"I don't know. I hope so. If I'm going to help him move on I need to figure out who he is, how he died, and how he came to be entombed in the secret room."

"And the other ghost?"

"Personally, I hope we don't cross paths. He sort of gave me the creeps. I know this is going to sound odd, but I sensed the boy was afraid of him."

"Can ghosts hurt each other?"

"I have no idea."

"I've seen movies where ghosts who are connected at death can relive the moment of their death over and over," Trevor joined in.

"Yeah, I've seen those too. Of course, movies are fiction. Still, there's something going on in that house."

"Again, I need to ask, should we really be doing this?" Mac asked. "No one knows where we are. It's dark, windy, and cold, and I bet the rain is going to start coming down a lot harder before we make it back to the car. What do we really hope to accomplish?"

"I don't know, but I think we're about to find out. Shadow just disappeared behind that large rock, and I seem to remember seeing a large rock when the boys showed us the entrance last night."

After Mac, Trevor, and I squeezed around the rock, we crawled through the small opening and then slid down the steep decline at the entrance. I remembered the boys telling us they couldn't get out this way when it rained, and because it seemed heavy rain was imminent, I knew we needed to make it a quick visit tonight. Once we reached where the passageway leveled off, we paused to get our bearings. Shadow stopped walking and the ghost of the child appeared. He looked frightened, just as he had the previous night, but when Shadow approached he smiled and bent down to hug him. I wondered if the cat and ghost could actually feel each other, though it didn't seem to matter; they were obviously happy to see each other.

I took a minute to decide on my approach. He might be dead, but he was still a child, and I didn't want to scare him off.

"My name is Alyson," I said in a soft voice. "These are my friends, Mac and Trevor."

The ghost faded away.

"We won't hurt you. You can trust us. We only want to help you. Will you let us?"

The boy reappeared.

"Are you here alone?"

The boy nodded.

"We want to help you move on, but you'll need to help us do that. Can you show us something that will help us understand what you need from us?"

The boy faded away again, but I waited. I had the feeling he was working his way up to trusting us. I supposed I understood his trepidation. Not only were we strangers, but I was probably the first person to see the boy since he died.

"Shadow can sense you're still here," I finally said when the boy failed to reappear. "He wants to help you too. He hopes you'll show us what you need. Can you do that?"

The boy reappeared. He turned and went down the passage, with Shadow following behind. When he came to the room where he'd been entombed he went through the door, which had been left open. He paused at one of the cabinets against the wall. The wooden boxes that had held the skeletons had been removed from the room. The open cabinet doors indicated the contents had been removed as well. I wasn't sure what the boy wanted us to see or find, but I approached the first cabinet and began to pull out the drawers, which all appeared to be empty. I had no idea if I was even on the right track, though the boy stood patiently, waiting, so I thought there must be something to find.

"Maybe there's a secret compartment or a false bottom," Trevor suggested.

I looked at the boy. "Are you sure it's here?"

He nodded.

I ran my hand slowly along the surface of every shelf, looking for whatever it was the boy wanted me to find. After a while I found a latch beneath the bottom shelf. When I pulled it a drawer popped out. Inside, I found several pads of paper that looked as if they'd been used by a child for drawing pictures. Just as I picked up the pads, the door to the passage slammed shut.

The boy disappeared.

"What the heck?" Mac said.

"I thought ghosts couldn't move objects," Trevor seconded.

"They can't. At least I don't think they can. It could have been a wind gust coming from the opening in the forest. Let's get that door open and get out of here."

It took our combined strength to get the door open, but eventually we managed to get it wide enough for us to squeeze through. I tucked the pads under my jacket, picked up Shadow, and headed back down the passage. I could hear the rain pounding on the surface of the forest floor as we neared the entrance. I just hoped we hadn't waited too long. The steep incline was slippery but not yet impassable, and we managed to make our way back into the dark forest.

"Okay, that was weird," Mac said when we were all out.

"Yeah, it was. Let's get out of here."

The walk back through the dark forest in the pouring rain was no picnic, but eventually, we made it back to the Jeep, where I turned on the defroster and the windshield wipers and drove toward town. I stopped at both Mac's and Trevor's so they could get dry clothes and then the three of us, along with Shadow, went to my house.

******

The pads were filled with drawings. Based on the skill level of the artist, I assumed they were those of a child. They were dark in nature, most of them revolving around death, bloody bodies, and monsters.

"These are really disturbing," I said aloud.

"They really are," Mac agreed. "Do you think our child ghost drew them before he died?"

I frowned. "He seems so sweet and shy, I'm having a hard time believing he would have been capable of drawing these dark images." I turned a page. "Take this one, for example. The images at the bottom look like animals of some sort. Maybe squirrels or cats. Every one of them has a knife sticking out of it and blood flowing from the wound. Whoever drew these was seriously disturbed. I didn't pick up that level of mental instability from the child ghost."

"Yet he led us to the drawings," Trevor pointed out. "And because his remains were in the room, it's likely he was murdered there. Maybe he was held as a hostage before he was killed. Maybe he saw and experienced horrible things that skewed his view of the world."

I really hoped not, but it seemed as good an explanation as any.

"Does anyone else think it's really strange that Woody hasn't come up with a missing persons report that matches the remains yet?" Mac asked. "If this kid was held as a hostage before he died someone must have been looking for him. He was just a kid. It makes no sense that he could just disappear and no one would notice."

"Joe and Jenny Jenkins lived in the house before Mr. Weston," Trevor reminded us. "They had foster kids. Maybe they were cruel to them. Maybe one of the kids died and they hid his remains."

"The kids in the foster care system are supposed to be monitored pretty closely," I responded. "If one of them just disappeared someone should have known about it."

"Alyson is right." Mac nodded. "A child in the foster care system shouldn't simply disappear without someone noticing. There has to be something else going on. Maybe the kid was a runaway, or maybe it was a parent who killed him. We don't even know for certain the person who hid the bodies lived in the house. The room was accessible from the forest, after all."

"Don't you think the person who lived in the house would know if someone else had access to the room?" I asked.

"Maybe," Mac answered. "Maybe not."

"The kids said Mr. Weston told them never to touch the door," Trevor said. "He wouldn't have done that if he didn't know what was behind it. He either was the killer or he was protecting the killer."

"I think Trevor's right," I said. "It does seem as if Mr. Weston had to have known what was in the room."

"Did you ever find out the cause of death for either of the victims?" Mac asked.

"No," I answered. "Woody didn't know the last time I spoke to him." I sat back in my chair and considered the situation. "We have to be missing something. We know there were the skeletons of two individuals hidden in a room at the end of a hidden passageway. We know one of the skeletons was a child's, the other an adult's, and based on the two ghosts I've seen, we're assuming the child was a boy of around ten when he died, the adult a male with a scary energy I didn't like in the least. Chan gave me two names and a date as a clue, so we're assuming the boy is Bobby and the man Julius, although it could be the other way around. We're also assuming the victims died twenty to thirty years ago, although we haven't received forensic confirmation of that."

"Even if the ME doesn't know cause of death yet he must have figured out the approximate time of death by now," Mac said. "I imagine it would be hard to tell TOD from bones, but I think there's a way to come up with at least a date range."

"Good point. I'll call Woody tomorrow to see if he'll tell me what he knows. We don't even know if they died at the same time."

"Do you think you can get more information from the child?" Trevor asked. "It seems like he's beginning to trust you, and he did show you where to find the drawings."

"Maybe," I answered. "But I can feel the boy is scared of the man, and I also sense the man doesn't want us snooping around."

"I wonder why that is?" Mac mused. "The guy's dead. We can't hurt him, so why does he feel threatened by our presence?"

"Good question."

"Maybe the man killed the child and then someone else killed him," Trevor speculated.

"Even if that's so, why would he care if we figured it out? It's not like we can send him to prison for murder. You'd think he'd want us to help him move on."

"But what if he doesn't want to move on?" Trevor asked.

I stopped to consider that. I supposed the man could be attached to something that was keeping him there. And he might not want us to help the child move on. Maybe it was even the child he was attached to. "So he sees us as a threat to an existence he's perfectly happy with," I said aloud. "That actually makes sense. The boy and the man are both trapped in the house. The boy seems frightened and appears to be motivated to move on, but the man seems to want us gone."

"We really do need to figure out who they were and what their relationship was to each other when they were alive," Mac said.

"I guess until we figure out the approximate date both victims died, as well as the reason they died, we're pretty much stuck," I admitted. "Maybe we should pick this up on Monday. I'll talk to Woody after school and we can meet up after that."

Chapter 9

Monday, October 23

For the first time in weeks I met Mac and Trevor for lunch in the school cafeteria instead of heading to the library for a nap. I felt like we'd hit a dead end in terms of figuring out who'd been hidden in the hidden passage, but I wasn't ready to give up either. What we needed was a new strategy, but first I wanted to solve Chelsea's stalker problem. The fact that the stalker seemed to be getting bolder was causing me a fair amount of alarm, even if Chelsea wasn't taking it quite as seriously.

"Here's what I know so far," Mac said as she nibbled on a plate of French fries. "As I already told Alyson," Mac directed her comment to Trevor, "there are three people with access to the student passwords: the principal, the teacher in charge of the computer lab, and the IT guy, who works for the district.

Someone is using a different student account each time an email is sent, so I have to assume the person sending the photos has access to all the student passwords."

"Remind me to change mine," Trevor commented.

"Won't help," Mac responded. "The passwords are stored in a file on the server and whoever has access to them has to have access to the whole file. If we could prove a breach we could get the administration to change the password to the file itself, but Chelsea doesn't want her dilemma brought to the attention of the school administrators. Alyson has agreed to honor her request for the time being. If, however, it appears she's in real danger, or if the photos become inappropriate, we'll need to tell Chelsea's parents what's going on despite her wishes."

"Okay, so how do we narrow things down?" I asked.

"I doubt that the principal, computer lab teacher, or district IT guy have been following Chelsea around, so we need to focus in on who might have obtained the password to the file from one of them at some point," Mac answered. "I found out that the password to the database was changed at the beginning of the school year, so that means the stalker would have had to gain access to the new password within the past six weeks. I thought about just asking the three people we know have access if they'd given it to anyone, but they'd want to know why I was asking, and short of spilling Chelsea's secret, I haven't come up with a good story."

"Were any of the emails Chelsea received sent from staff computers?" I asked.

"No. Chelsea's received ten emails over the course of the past two weeks. Seven of them were sent from the computer lab, two from the reference computer in the library, and one from the attendance office. Every student on campus has access to the computers in the library as well as the computer lab, and student aides have access to the computers in the attendance office, I'm thinking the stalker is a student aide."

"And how many student aides are there?" Trevor asked.

"Twelve, two for each period. The one email sent from the attendance office went out last week on Wednesday during the break between second and third period. I checked, and the two aides that day during second period were Miranda Portman and Art Dupree, and the two during third period were Sherry Vega and Donny Crier."

"It sounds like we need to have a chat with the four of them," Trevor stated.

"I'll need to fill Chelsea in. I promised I'd let her know if I needed to speak to anyone else about her situation." I turned and looked at Mac. "Is it possible that one of the other student aides could have popped in and sent the email even if it wasn't their time to work?"

"Sure. The staff trusts the aides and they're used to seeing them around. I doubt they would question it if one from a different period popped in for a minute. It makes sense to start with the four who were actually supposed to be there, however."

"I think I saw Chelsea pop into the locker room. I'll go fill her in and if she agrees we'll track down the four aides."

When I arrived in the locker room Chelsea was standing at the mirror touching up her makeup. Given the amount of time she invested in making herself look perfect, I wondered how she ever managed to get anything else done.

"So, did you find my stalker?" Chelsea asked without even pausing to look in my direction.

"Not yet, but we're narrowing things down. We know the emails you were sent all came from different student accounts. That means your stalker has access to the student passwords."

Chelsea paused and looked at me. "You aren't saying my stalker is that creepy Mr. Pruitt from the computer lab, are you?"

"No, we don't think it's him, although at this point we aren't ruling anyone out. The computers that were used to send the emails came from either the computer lab, the library, or the attendance office. Our theory is that one of the student aides managed to get their hands on the passwords. The next step is to talk to them to see what we can find out."

Chelsea frowned. "Talk to them? Does that mean you'll have to tell them I have a stalker?"

"We thought we'd just say we're looking in to unauthorized emails sent from the attendance office. There may come a time when we'll be forced to be more specific. And the more people we speak to, the greater the odds that a staff member will find out. I really think, given the complexity of the situation, you should talk to your parents."

"I can't. My dad can be really overprotective. If he knew what was going on he'd probably lock me in my room, which would severely curtail my ability to live my life. I have cheerleading practice all week, a game on Friday, and the Hayride on Saturday. I'm not going to miss out on everything because some creep is getting his jollies following me around. Find out who's doing this, but keep my name out of it."

"We will for now, but I'm not promising anything. Did you get any new photos over the weekend?"

Chelsea nodded. She took out her phone and pulled up her texts then handed it to me. There were two new photos. One was of her standing near the bleachers during the game on Friday. She had a bottle of water in her hand and there was a pile of athletic bags nearby, so I assumed she'd stashed her belongings, along with those of the other cheerleaders, near the base of the bleachers. The other photo showed her climbing out of her car in front of her house. She had on a pair of jeans and a T-shirt, so I assumed she'd just run an errand.

"Do you remember where you were coming from when this photo was taken?" I asked.

"The pharmacy. My mom's allergies were acting up and her doctor called in a prescription. That photo was taken Saturday morning at around eight-thirty."

I didn't like the idea that someone was following Chelsea around at eight-thirty in the morning on a weekend. "Are you usually up and about that early in the morning?" I asked.

"On a Saturday? Never. But my mom really felt bad and my dad had gone golfing, so I got up and ran the errand. Most of the time I sleep until noon on Saturday unless we have a game."

"So far, all the emails you've received have been sent on weekdays and all the texts on weekends. That makes sense because the emails have been sent from school. We haven't had any luck tracing the burner cell the texts have been sent from, but I suggest you block the number and then see what happens. I'm curious if the stalker will begin sending the texts from a different phone number, or if he or she will stop texting altogether."

Chelsea shrugged. "Okay. That's fine by me."

I punched in the information to block the number on Chelsea's phone.

"So what now?" she asked.

"We're going to speak to the student aides. If you get any additional texts or emails let me know right away. I'm hoping the stalker will make a mistake that will allow Mac to hone in on them."

Chelsea sighed. "Okay. I'll let you know if I get any more photos, but find this guy. I hate being watched and I want my life back."

Mac and Trevor were chatting with a couple of friends when I returned to the lunchroom. I made a comment about needing to follow up on a project and they said their good-byes and followed me out into the common area, which provided outdoor tables that overlooked the sea. During the spring it was packed with students, but now there was a chill in the air, so we were the only ones outside.

"I spoke to Chelsea. She's adamant about wanting us to keep her name out of it, but I figured we could just speak to the student aides about unauthorized emails being sent from the attendance office and maybe their reactions will give us some insight as to whether they know anything. There are four names on our list. Miranda's in my class next period, so I'll try to pull her aside."

"Sorry." Mac tilted her head. "I need to leave for my internship in about five minutes, but if you don't get to everyone today I can help tomorrow, and I might be able to work on the cell phone some more if I get a break."

"I blocked the number from Chelsea's phone. I'm interested to see how the stalker reacts. Of course, the texts all came in on the weekends, so chances are Chelsea will only receive emails today anyway. It does seem the student-aide angle is our best bet, so I think that's what we should focus our energy on."

"I have math next period, then football," Trevor said. "I probably won't see any of the four student aides, but if I do run into them I'll see what they know."

"I'm going to head over to the police station after school," I told them. "Do you want to come by later this afternoon? Maybe we can regroup and figure out where we stand on both of our mysteries."

They agreed, and I headed to my fifth-period class. I hoped Miranda would show up early so I could catch her for a minute before class started.

"Miranda," I called out as I hurried down the hallway before she had a chance to go into the room.

Miranda stopped, turned, and waited for me. "Hey, Alyson. What's up?"

"I need to ask you about an article I'm writing for the school newspaper," I improvised as I looked carefully at her face, hoping I could read her reaction to my next words. "It seems there's been a number of unauthorized emails being sent from the attendance office." Okay, I was exaggerating; there'd only been one, but I wanted to make it sound like the problem was more widespread. "I know you work in the office and I wondered if you'd seen or heard anything that might help me track down the source."

Miranda looked surprised but not alarmed. "No. I hadn't heard a thing. All the aides know that sending emails from the computers in the office is against the rules. In fact, the only time we're allowed to use the computers at all is to look up student attendance and class information if we need to pass on a message."

"You work in the office during second period?"

Miranda nodded. "That's right. Art Dupree and I both cover second period."

"Have you ever seen Art using the computers when he might not have been authorized to do so?"

Miranda laughed. "Art? Surely you don't think Art is the student aide you're looking for?"

"Not specifically. I'm just asking around about all the aides at this point."

The first bell rang, so I had maybe a minute more before Miranda headed inside.

"Art would never break the rules. I mean *never*. He's one of those people who's overly fixated on the rules. The other day I used a paper clip to attach a parent's note to an attendance report and he almost went crazy. Sure, we're supposed to *staple* parents' notes to attendance reports so they aren't separated, but I couldn't find the stapler and there was a jar of paper clips sitting on one of the desks, so I was making do."

I narrowed my gaze. "You said Art went crazy. What do you mean by that?"

"Okay, maybe *crazy* is too strong a word, but he grabbed the things I'd paper clipped together off the top of the pile and spent the next several minutes lecturing me about the rules and the reason we need to follow them while he searched the office for a stapler. The guy is very rigid. I'm pretty sure he has some sort of obsessive compulsive disorder. I wish they'd assign me to another period so I could work with someone else, but the only one left when I applied to be an aide was third, with Art. I think the only reason the spot was even open was because no one wants to work with him."

Miranda turned to walk to our classroom and I fell into step beside her. "Why don't you just drop the aide gig and take another class?"

"My grade point average is in the toilet. I need an easy A, and being an aide is an easy A as long as you show up and do a passable job."

I guess that explained why there was usually a waiting list of students wanting to be aides. "Okay, well, thanks for the insight. I may try to speak to Art, but it sounds like he most likely isn't the student I'm looking for. Do you have any idea who might not have a problem with sending unauthorized emails?"

"You might want to talk to Donny Crier. He's in the office during third period. I don't know if you know him, but he seems to be one of those people who think the rules don't apply to him. I don't even know why they let him be an aide, except that his mom is on the school board, so she probably called in a favor. Donny is in my English class and he already has so many missing assignments, there's no way he's going to pass. I'm sure he wanted to be a student aid to get his overall GPA up to something that might justify letting him graduate."

I took my seat just as the teacher asked everyone to settle down. I hadn't had the sense that Miranda had lied to me, and she really didn't seem to know about any unauthorized emails, so I doubted she was the person we were looking for. Besides, I couldn't think of a single reason Miranda would be stalking Chelsea. Uptight Art and Slacker Donny, however, were another thing altogether. The more I thought about it, the more I could see either of them being the stalker.

Chapter 10

As planned, I headed over to the police station after school. I hoped Woody would not only be in but that he would be alone and willing to talk to me. If we were going to make any progress in helping the ghosts of the skeletons move on, we needed to figure out who they were and when and how they died, and I suspected their time of death would correlate to the date Chan had provided. Though for all I knew, the date could be related to something else entirely.

"Ms. Prescott," Woody greeted me.

"Alyson."

"Of course. What can I do for you, Alyson?"

I walked up to the counter Woody was standing behind and leaned against it. "I'm here to find out if you have any news. The others and I have been curious about who the skeletons belong to and their cause of death."

"I'm not sure I should be discussing this with a civilian, but you did help me when it came to the matter of the child fingerprints and my sense is I can trust you not to speak of the matter out of turn."

I pretended to turn a key over my lips. "Except for sharing what I know with Mac and Trevor, my lips are sealed."

"As you know, the remains we have to work with aren't much. The cause of death doesn't appear to be anything that would readily show up on the bones, such as a gunshot wound or blunt force trauma. Without the organs, it's going to be hard to determine exactly what happened. If it turns out that the cause of death was something like asphyxiation or poisoning it could be almost impossible to determine. We're still working on it, though, and we may still catch a break."

"And the identities of the victims?"

"Still unknown at this time. We ran missing persons reports using the approximate age of each and the approximate year they died. So far, we've come up with absolutely nothing. Again, we're still working on it, but I think if we're going to make an identification, we'll need additional information that we don't have right now. I'm in the process of pulling together everything I can find about Mr. Weston, but so far, he really does seem to be nothing more than a nice old man who lived alone and mostly kept to himself. By all accounts he lived a quiet life and, at least during the thirty years he lived in that house, he had few if any friends."

"Except for the boys who had a hangout on the second story of his house," I said.

"Yes. Except for them. I'll admit his willingness to let the boys come and go as they chose doesn't fit what I've been able to dig up about him."

"Did he ever marry or have children?"

"He married a woman named Velina Horn in 1963. They had one child, a son, who died in 1983 when he was only nine. Velina fell into a depression and committed suicide six months later. Mr. Weston appears to have lived alone from that point on."

"How sad. I know he bought the house in 1985. Do you know where he lived before that?"

"In a small farming community in Kansas. Interestingly, he was a doctor and retired just prior to moving to Cutter's Cove."

"And he never practiced here?"

"No. And he didn't refer to himself as a doctor at all. As far as I can tell, he went by Mr. Weston from the moment he moved here. He lived alone in the house, rarely venturing out."

"It seems he lived a tragic life, but that doesn't explain how two bodies ended up entombed in a room in his house." I paused, considering the situation. "There has to be something else we haven't stumbled upon. Not only did Mr. Weston literally have skeletons in his closet, but it seems odd that an educated man who'd dedicated his life to helping others would isolate himself the way he did in his later years. I understand he suffered a huge loss with the death of a son and a wife in such a short period of time, but wouldn't he have wanted to get out and rejoin the living after a period of grieving?"

"I agree. There's definitely something that isn't adding up."

I tapped my fingers on the counter as I thought. "And why buy such a huge house? Caleb told me it's over five thousand square feet. Why would a man who was alone in the world buy a large home unless he had plans to entertain or even eventually remarry? Have you spoken to his neighbors?"

"Not yet, but I plan to. The house is at the end of the road, bordered by the forest, but there are a couple of farms along the same road. If nothing else someone might have seen something."

"Let's go now."

"*Let's*?" Woody asked.

******

The farm closest to the Weston property was owned by an older couple, Melvin and Maude Moody. The land had once been used to grow strawberries, but the Moodys were no longer able to maintain the crop; other than a small garden they kept for personal use, the land had been allowed to return to a natural state. The small home we found at the end of the drive was weathered, but the yard was neatly tended, as was the bright red barn that stood off to one side. Large hens roamed, while several pigs, a couple of goats, and a handful of dairy cows were housed in pens beyond the barn.

"I love it. The whole place is so quaint."

Woody stopped the car and turned off the engine. "Remember, I'll do the talking."

"I won't forget," I assured him. "You're the cop, so you're in charge."

As we got out of the car, a pair of border collies came from the back of the lot to greet us with warning barks but wagging tails.

"Sampson and Delilah, whatever are you going on about?" I heard a woman call from inside the house.

I waved at the gray-haired woman, who stepped out onto the covered front porch with a friendly smile on her face.

"Can I help you?" she asked Woody as he walked toward her.

"I'm Officer Baker and this is Alyson Prescott. We'd like to speak to you about Eliston Weston."

"He's dead."

"Yes, ma'am, we know that. But there have been some developments at his house, so we're speaking to his neighbors."

She opened the screen door. "Well, come on in, then. I just made some fresh-squeezed lemonade. Have a seat in the kitchen and I'll call my husband to join us."

Woody and I sat down at the small dining table in the sunny yellow kitchen. There were bright green plants around the room and blue and white canisters decorated the kitchen counter. The scent of pumpkin and cinnamon lingered in the air, and I was willing to bet the loaf shapes under white kitchen towels were pumpkin bread.

Mrs. Moody returned to the room with a gentleman about her age and poured four glasses of lemonade before joining us at the table.

"How can we help you?" Mr. Moody asked.

"As I'm sure you know, the house at the end of the road is being used by the high school for their annual Haunted Hayride. During decorating for the event, Ms. Prescott and her friends found a locked room located off a hidden passageway. Inside the room were two skeletons."

"Oh my," Mrs. Moody said, her hand over her mouth.

"You're saying Weston had two human skeletons hidden up there in that house?" Mr. Moody asked.

"Yes," Woody confirmed. "We estimate the individuals would have died approximately twenty-five years ago. Did you live here back then?"

"Sure." Mr. Moody nodded. "Maude and I have lived here since we married more than fifty years ago."

"Did you speak often to Mr. Weston before his death two years ago?" Woody asked.

"Not often. We'd wave to each other if we passed on the road and he came over when my dang-nabbed tractor rolled over on me and patched me up."

"And when was that?" Woody asked.

"I guess it's been about fifteen years now. The man used to be a doctor, and I think he must have been a good one."

"Had Mr. Weston lived alone in the house the whole time he owned it?" I asked, even though I was supposed to let Woody do all the talking.

"No." Mr. Moody shook his head. "There was a boy who stayed at the house for a while after Weston moved in. He wasn't quite right in the head, so Weston kept him inside most of the time, but he managed to sneak out every now and again, and Weston had to go out and look for him."

"How old was the boy?" I asked.

"I guess around fourteen or fifteen. His name was Jojo, or at least that was what Weston called him. I seem to remember Weston telling me that Jojo was his sister's kid and he was helping her out by letting him stay at the house while she was away."

"And how long ago was this?" Woody asked.

"I remember the boy started coming around a few years after Weston moved in. I didn't see him often, but Weston came looking for him several times over a four- or five-year period. At some point he stopped coming to visit. I think the tantrums got to be too much for the doc as the boy got older."

"Did you ever see any younger boys in the area?" I asked. "Boys who would have been about ten?"

Mr. Moody shook his head. "Not back then. There've been some kids hanging around the past few years. I think they live in the neighborhood on the far side of the forest. Weston seemed to enjoy their company, so he encouraged them to visit."

"Did Mr. Weston have any other regular visitors that you know of?" Woody asked.

"No. He was always real friendly when I ran into him on the road, but he liked his privacy. I can respect that."

We spoke to the Moodys for a while longer and then returned to Woody's car. "Are you thinking what I am?" I asked once we were seat-belted inside.

"If you're thinking Mr. Weston's nephew is the male skeleton, then yes."

"It makes sense. Mr. Weston had already suffered a great tragedy with the loss of his wife and son. He came to Cutter's Cove to find a quiet place to heal, and then his sister asked him to help with her mentally challenged child. Mr. Weston agreed, but the boy wasn't an easy teen to deal with. He would sneak out, and I suppose we can assume got into a certain amount of trouble. Mr. Weston got into a conflict with the boy and somehow, he died. Maybe he fell down the stairs or fell and hit his head."

"Wait." I stopped Woody. "I had you up until that last part. You told me there was no skeletal evidence of trauma."

Woody scratched his chin. "That's true. The ME didn't find any broken bones."

"And what about the sister? If the male skeleton in the box was this nephew of Weston's, why did she let her brother leave his body there? Wouldn't she want to give her son a proper burial?"

"I suppose she could have been protecting her brother," Woody answered.

"But if the death of the teen was an accident would he need protecting?"

"Maybe he killed the boy in a fit of rage." Woody sighed. "I guess the next step is to track down the sister to see what she can tell us."

I narrowed my gaze. "It seems as if, given the circumstances, Mr. Weston's next of kin would have been contacted right away."

"I didn't find any other than the nephew who now owns the property," Woody informed me. "The nephew lives in Italy and claims to have never met his uncle. His mother was Weston's sister. She went abroad when she was in college and met the man she eventually married. She moved to Italy when she was just twenty-two and delivered her only child, a son, when she was twenty-six. She died when she was just twenty-nine, without ever having introduced her brother to her family. According to the nephew, he was as shocked as anyone when he was named as the sole heir to a farm owned by a man he'd never had any contact with."

"If Weston played host to a different nephew after moving to Cutter's Cove he must have had another sister," I said.

"Yeah. It's odd that the nephew didn't know that. I'll do some digging to see what I can find out. In the meantime, let's check with the neighbor just south of here before we head back."

I smiled at Woody. "Sounds good, partner."

Chapter 11

As it turned out, the other neighbor, while very nice, had only lived in the area for fourteen years and, based on the estimation of the ME, the victims we'd found would already have been dead. The neighbor did say Mr. Weston was a quiet sort who liked to keep to himself and never really caused any problems or made any noise, so in his opinion, he was a good neighbor to have. He added that he had witnessed Mr. Weston taking walks along Harbinger Lane late at night, which had seemed odd to him. Woody and I discussed the fact that someone who wanted to avoid social interactions with others might choose to walk after his neighbors had turned in for the night; given what we knew about Mr. Weston, his late-night excursions didn't necessarily mean anything.

The more I learned about the mysterious Mr. Weston, the sorrier I felt for him, unless, of course, he actually had killed two people in cold blood. I thought about the boy who haunted the house and wondered once again who he was and how he came to be there.

After we returned to the police station, I said good-bye to Woody, who promised to call me after he located the second sister. I needed to get home to meet with Mac and Trevor, but I had to admit I'd been having the best time with Woody that afternoon. I appreciated his willingness to work with me rather than simply shutting me out, as most cops would have done. It somewhat made sense to me that the adult remains we'd found could have belonged to Mr. Weston's nephew, but that still didn't explain the skeleton of the child or how the nephew died or why no one seemed to have noticed he was missing.

"I may have a lead on Chelsea's stalker," Mac informed me after we'd settled in around the dining table to work on our homework and discuss both mysteries.

"Okay. What do you have?" I asked.

"After we spoke at lunch I decided to do a little fishing. I dug into the social media accounts of all twelve student aides to see if I could pick out anyone who might be using a digital camera with a telephoto lens rather than just a cell phone, as most of the kids in school do."

"And...?"

"Karina Hinton is a photographer for the school newspaper and she's also a student aide fifth period. I don't know if she'd have any reason to stalk Chelsea, but it seems she would have the equipment and opportunity. Not only does her stint as a student aide give her access to the attendance office but her role for the newspaper gives her access to areas of the school not all students have."

I paused to picture who Karina was. Being new to the school, I didn't know the names of all the students. "Karina is the girl with the long red hair who usually does the interviews for the theater events?"

"Yeah, that's her," Mac confirmed.

Trevor took a sip of his soda, then raised a hand as if he had something to add. I glanced in his direction. "She also helps out in the computer lab from time to time," he said. "I think she's sort of like a teacher's aide or something. I don't know that Mr. Pruitt would give her access to the student passwords, but he's left her alone with the class on a couple of occasions, so she could have gone through his computer and found the passwords."

"She is pretty smart," Mac admitted. "If she had access to Pruitt's computer and he wasn't careful with his own security she may have been able to get hold of them."

I frowned. "I don't know Karina well at all and it does seem she may have had the access she needed to send the photos to Chelsea, but she seems like a serious student with her eye on the future. I don't think she's the sort to be in to the whole social hierarchy thing. I can't imagine her wanting to spend hours and hours every week stalking Chelsea."

"Alyson has a point," Mac admitted.

"Who else do you have?" I asked.

"Art Dupree. He's a second-period student aide and has photos posted on his Facebook and Instagram pages from his trip to Alaska last year. Many of them were obviously taken with a telephoto lens."

"I spoke to Miranda today. She seemed certain that nerdy Art would never break the rules and access information he'd been forbidden from looking at, but in my experience, it's often the socially unable students who make the best suspects when it comes to bullying from a distance, which stalking obviously is."

"The guy's a strange dude," Trevor agreed. "And I've seen him ogling Chelsea. I'd be willing to bet he's our guy."

"I'll chat with him tomorrow. Who else do we have?" I asked.

"Mike Walker. He isn't only the district's IT guy, he's also an amateur photographer who's sold some of his wildlife photos from around the world."

I was beginning to get a bad feeling about this. "So, this IT guy would have access to all three computers used *and* the student passwords. You don't actually think...?" The thought was so disturbing, I found myself unable to complete my sentence.

"I hope not, but according to his Facebook bio he's single and fairly young—just twenty-four. I guess he could have noticed Chelsea while he was on campus. He's a college graduate with a degree in technology, so I don't know why he would even mess around with a high school student, but I suppose there are all sorts of weirdos out there."

"I think we should have a talk with this guy," Trevor said. He balled a fist and hit the palm of his other hand with it. "Actually, I think *I* should have a talk with this guy."

"Don't go all Rambo on us. We don't have any proof he's the stalker," I countered. "All we really know so far is that he likes to take photos, has a nice camera, and has access to the computers and passwords." I looked at Mac. "Were there any photos posted to this man's social media accounts that seemed like the ones Chelsea's been receiving?"

"No. Nothing really stood out when it came to subject matter."

"So how can we narrow our suspect pool down to one?" Trevor asked.

"I'll talk to Karina and Art tomorrow," I offered. "If neither seems like the stalker we'll regroup and decide what to do. If it does look like Mike is our guy I think we should consider telling Chelsea's parents."

"I agree," Trevor said. "In fact, I think if an adult is involved we should go to the cops."

"Maybe," I agreed.

"Speaking of cops, how'd your meeting with Woody go?" Mac asked.

I filled both Mac and Trevor in on the new information I had gathered that day. I hoped Woody would call back that afternoon with news about the sister who was unaccounted for and maybe we could put this mystery to bed. It was less than a week until the Hayride, which Caleb and crew were still hoping to hold if the cops would release the house in time to get the decorating done. Caleb had let me know Wednesday, the 25th, was their drop-dead date. If they didn't have access by the time school let out then, they were going to officially cancel the Hayride and refund the money for all the presold tickets.

"Are we sure there isn't another farm in the area that will work?" Trevor asked. "I already laid down a month's allowance on a horrifyingly gory costume.

"I asked, but Caleb said none came to mind. I told him if I thought of anything I'd let him know."

"What about the Providence place?" Mac asked. "It's not a farm that would allow for a hayride, but it's a big old spooky-looking place just outside of town. The house is three stories tall, I think, and it's on a large piece of land that just happens to back up to an old cemetery. Instead of a hayride, everyone can walk through the Haunted Cemetery. A narrated event could be followed by the party, which is the reason most people go anyway."

"Do you think the town would allow the school to use the cemetery for something like that?" I asked.

"The cemetery is outside of the town limits and there are no burials there anymore. I suppose the school would still need to get a permit or permission of some sort. Maybe from the county? There's a path that someone roped off at some point, probably to protect the old graves. It would seem to me that as long as a guide kept people on the trail the gravesites themselves wouldn't suffer any ill effects."

"I think it's worth looking in to," Trevor said. "A walk through a real graveyard sounds about as spooky as it gets."

"I'll call Caleb. If he's open to the idea I guess it wouldn't hurt to check it out, although we don't have a lot of time to get permission if the land is owned by the county."

"Maybe it's privately owned," Trevor suggested.

"I can look it up," Mac offered.

I went into the kitchen to get snacks for everyone while Mac set up her computer. I was trying to decide between chips and dip and cheese and crackers when my cell rang.

"Hey, Woody. I was hoping you'd call. Did you find the second sister?"

"No. I did a thorough search that came up with birth certificates for Eliston Weston from 1935 and Sylvia Weston from 1942. I couldn't find a single reference to a third child."

"Are we thinking the teen Weston watched out for was Sylvia's?"

"Not unless it was a secret birth. Sylvia moved to Italy in 1965. She had a son in 1968 and she died in 1971. The son she bore is the nephew who inherited the property. By all accounts, he's never been to the States."

I paused. "So who was the teen the Moodys remembered?"

"I'm digging further into Mr. Weston's family tree, but it seems that except for him, people in his family died young. It appears neither of his parents lived to see him graduate college, and all four grandparents met with early deaths."

"It seems like the family was cursed."

"If I believed in curses I'd agree."

I hung up with Woody and returned to the dining room with the chips and dip. It seemed it was becoming a junk food sort of day. After I set the food on the table I filled the others in on what the police had learned.

"The teen Mr. Weston took care of must not have been an actual nephew," Trevor said. "Maybe he was the child of a friend of the family or a nephew by marriage. Did his wife have siblings?"

"Good question," I realized. "You guys help yourself to the chips. I'm going to call Woody back to see if he checked the wife's family tree."

Woody didn't answer when I called so I left a message asking him to call me back. When I returned to the dining area Mac and Trevor were both looking at her computer screen.

"What'd you find?" I asked.

"The Providence house is owned by the Providence family, one of the founding families in the area. The land, as well as the adjoining graveyard, are currently owned by family members living on the East Coast. The cemetery was only used from the late eighteen hundreds through the early nineteen hundreds. I can find the contact information if Caleb decides he's interested in the house. I don't know if the family will allow the property to be used for a party, but it could be worth a phone call to find out."

I hesitated. "I didn't realize the house was that old. It might be a historical landmark."

"Actually, the house itself is only around fifty years old. The original structure burned down and was rebuilt in the 1960s. The last family to live in it moved away more than twenty years ago, so I assume the place isn't in great shape, but again, it wouldn't hurt to check it out."

I called Caleb, who was open to a backup plan. He planned to drive by, and if it looked like it would work he'd call Mac for more information on the family who owned the place. He still hoped it would work out to use the house on Harbinger Lane because a lot of the work to ready it had already been done, but the Providence house would likely be better than no house at all.

"So, do we focus on our English paper or our physics homework?" Mac asked once we'd determined we'd done what we could on both mysteries.

"Physics," I said. "I've gotten behind and really need to get caught up before the test next week."

"I don't have physics or Advance Placement English, so I think I'll head out," Trevor announced. "If anything comes up you girls can call me."

"Okay," I said. "Maybe we should…" My words were interrupted by the ringing of my phone. I answered the call, then turned back to them. "That was Caleb. His mother made dinner reservations with an old friend of the family and wants him to join them. He wants to know if we can do a drive-by of the Providence house."

Mac shrugged. "Sure, but I'm not the one who has physics assignments to make up."

"That's okay; I can do them later. Trevor?"

"I'm in. Checking out a spooky house sounds like a lot more fun than homework anyway."

"I'll drive," I offered. "I'm not sure where it is, so one of you will have to navigate."

Chapter 12

By the time we set out for the Providence house the sun was setting. Mac seemed to know exactly where to go, so I followed her directions, turning onto the highway and heading out of town. I still had flashlights in the cargo area of my Jeep, so even if the sky grew darker before we arrived I knew we could get a look at the place to determine the likelihood it would work for the fund-raiser.

"If you want to get a look at the graveyard there's a sharp left once you turn into the drive," Mac informed me.

"I'd like to see it," Trevor said. "In fact, I'm more interested in the graveyard than the house. We'll have a hard time selling the event without the Hayride unless we can step up the creep factor another way."

"Caleb said to take photos of everything and forward them to him, along with our general impression of the place," I answered.

As we neared the drive for the house and graveyard, Mac warned me to slow down a bit. She hadn't been out in this area since she was a child, so she needed to watch for the drive, which was most likely overgrown with weeds.

"I think it's just up the road after you pass the old pasture fence." Mac pointed in the direction I needed to go.

"I see it," I said as I put my foot on the brake. The dirt drive was in pretty bad shape but not impassable even for a regular car and certainly not for my four-wheel drive. Years of rain and the absence of regular grading made for a rough road with a lot of ruts, so I slowed down to no more than five miles an hour.

"The road to the graveyard should be just up ahead," Mac said. "I remember it being a sharp turn, so we'll need to watch for it."

"I see it, just beyond that rusted bike frame," Trevor announced.

I made the turn onto the road, which was in even worse shape than the main drive. "I don't know about this," I said. "The road is really rough. A lot of cars would have trouble navigating some of these ruts and we don't have time to grade the road."

"Yeah, it's a lot worse than I remember," Mac admitted.

There was a clearing just in front of us, so I pulled over and parked. The sky had darkened a bit, but the stone grave markers were still visible. I grabbed three flashlights from the cargo area and handed one each to Mac and Trevor.

"The place does have the spooky feel I was hoping for," Trevor said.

I found I had to agree. The area around the graveyard was barren except for a single tree that was completely devoid of leaves. The tree groaned as the bare branches dipped and swayed as the tall grass blew in the steady breeze. The cemetery itself was bordered by an iron fence that had once been painted white, though little of the color remained after years of exposure to the sun and other elements. The path through the gravestones was roped off, as Mac remembered, but the path, like the drive, was rutted with tall weeds that would need to be knocked down before the school could possibly use it.

"I don't think this is going to work," I said once again.

"Let's walk through anyway," Trevor urged. "We drove all the way out here."

Mac and I followed Trevor as he entered the graveyard through the rusted gate that hung from one hinge and looked as if it hadn't been functional for a lot of years.

"Generally, I enjoy walking through old graveyards, but this one seems to have a lot of children," Mac said as she shone her flashlight on the gravestones, some of which were raised, others little more than a slab of cement in the ground. "This baby was only four months old when she died, and here's the grave of her two-year-old sister. Talk about tragic: to lose one child must be the most difficult thing a person can go through, but to lose two children and both when they were so young. I'm not sure how you'd deal with that."

I shone my flashlight on the grave markers, agreeing the place was pretty depressing. At least a third of the souls buried here had died before they were ten. "I guess life was hard back then. There were a lot of diseases that afflicted children. I'm sure accidents claimed a lot of lives as well."

"Okay, this just segued from fun and sort of spooky to a total downer," Trevor complained.

"Yeah." Mac sighed. "The fun has gone out of the adventure. We came here to look at the house, which is just up ahead. Let's check it out and then get out of here. Suddenly physics homework doesn't sound so bad after all."

The minute the house came into view I knew it was the house from my dream. I wanted to scream, I wanted to flee, but all I did was stand perfectly still and stare at it.

"The porch is rotted through," Trevor said. I was sure he hadn't noticed the fact that I had stopped following.

"Are you okay?" Mac asked.

I simply stared. I didn't answer, didn't make a single movement.

"Do you see something?" Mac took my hand in hers and gave it a gentle squeeze. "Should we go?"

I nodded ever so slightly.

"Let's go," Mac called to Trevor. "The house is obviously a bust and I have a lot of homework. We'll call Caleb later to let him know."

Trevor looked in to one of the windows, shrugged, and headed back to where Mac and I were standing. "It's totally dark inside. I couldn't see a thing."

Mac gently took my hand and pulled me along beside her. Trevor chatted about the upcoming football game the entire way back through the cemetery, so he at least hadn't noticed the weirdness of my response to the house.

"Why don't you drive back?" Mac said to Trevor. "I think Alyson has a headache."

Trevor looked at me with a question in his eyes.

"Yeah," I said softly. "I think that would be best."

I sat in the backseat while Mac and Trevor chatted in the front. The drive home passed in a blur, and when we arrived I told my friends I was tired and planned to go in and get to bed early. Mac was clearly concerned, but she'd ridden to my house with Trevor, so after I hugged her and assured her I was fine she reluctantly left.

I headed inside and went directly up to my room. All I really wanted to do was to climb into my bed and pull the covers over my head, but I knew in my heart I needed to go back. I'd been having the dream for a reason. Chan had said the door represented the barrier between what I knew and what I needed to know. He'd indicated that the answers I sought would be found only after I conquered my fear and went inside.

Chan hadn't said anything about entering the house alone, so I grabbed Tucker and Shadow, left a note for my mom should she return home before I got back, and headed back to my Jeep. My heart was pounding and my palms sweating as I turned the key in the ignition. I fought the urge to run as I slowly shifted into Drive and started slowly down the driveway that connected the house to the Coast Highway. The sky had darkened even more and the only light, other than the headlights, were from the stars overhead. I glanced at the sea to my right and tried to permit the crashing of the waves to calm my jangled nerves. By the time I reached the deeply rutted dirt drive leading to the house I was almost numb with terror. The house was completely dark when I pulled up and stopped in front of it.

We hadn't checked the door when we'd been here before, but I knew it would be open. Just as I knew something or someone would be waiting on the other side. My legs felt weak and shaky as I climbed from the driver's side seat. I opened the back door and Tucker and Shadow jumped to the ground. I stood for a long time staring at the house, trying all the while to work up the courage to take a step forward.

You can do this.

I closed my eyes, swallowed hard, and took one step forward. I opened my eyes and forced myself take another step, and then another, until I was standing at the foot of the steps.

The dream is yours to conquer. I could hear Chan's voice in my mind. He'd said he would be there with me when the time came for me to slay my dragons, and somehow, I knew in my heart he was there now.

I placed one foot on the first step. I bit my lip so hard it began to bleed, but still I didn't give in to the urge to flee. I slowly lifted my other foot and placed it on the second step. Only two more, I coached myself, as I looked toward the dark door from my dream.

Shadow stood at the door, but Tucker was at my side. He licked my hand, which seemed to give me the courage I needed to conquer the final two steps. Once I arrived at the doorway I paused again. Shadow wove his way through my legs, purring so loudly I was certain if there was evil waiting for me, his offer of comfort would have quelled it before I entered.

I placed my hand on the door handle and slowly turned it. My heart felt like it was going to punch its way clear through my chest. My breath was coming in short, shallow intervals, and I began to feel the dizziness I'd experienced in my dream.

The dream is yours to conquer. Chan's voice echoed through my mind.

I slowly pushed the door open a mere inch at a time. The interior of the house was dark, so the only thing that greeted me through the opening was blackness. I held my flashlight firmly in one hand, clinging to Tucker's collar with the other. I took a breath, opened the door a bit wider, and took a step inside.

I let go of Tucker's collar and turned on the flashlight.

Oh God!

******

I must have passed out because the next thing I knew I was lying on the dusty floor and Tucker was licking my face. I slowly sat up and looked around the room. Every inch of every wall was completely covered with photos of me. Some of them were from as recently as five months ago; others had been taken of Amanda when I lived that life back in New York.

"Oh my God," Trevor said from behind me.

I turned to find both Mac and Trevor standing in the doorway.

"We called you when we got to my place. You didn't answer, and we had a feeling you were coming back," Mac explained. "This is the house from your dream."

I nodded and stood up.

"Does someone want to tell me what's going on?" Trevor demanded.

I glanced at Mac, who lifted a brow but didn't say anything.

"I've been having dreams about this place," I said aloud. "Terrible dreams, more like nightmares."

Trevor took several steps forward. He put his hands on my upper arms and looked me in the eye. "What's going on? Who took all these photos?"

"I don't know," I said.

"Do you think Chelsea's stalker is after you too?"

I shook my head. "No. It's not that."

Trevor used a finger to wipe a tear from my cheek. "Then what?"

I froze. I knew in my heart I should tell Trevor the truth, but I was scared. The more people who knew the truth, the more danger they and I were in.

"Alyson, what is it?" Trevor demanded again. "Do you know who took these photos?"

I nodded.

"Okay, then, who? And, more importantly, why?"

I took a deep breath and then answered. "My name isn't Alyson Prescott. It's Amanda Parker. Or at least it was. Technically, Amanda is dead."

Trevor frowned. "Huh?"

"Prior to moving to Cutter's Cove, I lived in New York. My best friend and I witnessed a gangland murder. She was killed by the men responsible for the murder and I was put into witness protection."

Trevor took a step back. He glanced at Mac. "You don't seem surprised."

"Mac knows," I answered.

I watched helplessly as pain crossed Trevor's face.

"I wanted to tell you. I almost did a million times, but I've been sworn to secrecy. My life is in danger.

My mother's life is in danger. I didn't want to put you in danger as well."

"You trusted Mac enough to tell her the truth, but you didn't trust me?"

"It's not like that," I cried.

"I snooped through Alyson's drawers when I spent the night at her house shortly after we met," Mac explained. "I found photos of Amanda in New York. Alyson didn't tell me because she trusts me more than she trusts you; she told me because I found out on my own."

Trevor walked across the room. He hit the wall and then bowed his head. I should have told him sooner. Now he'd never forgive me.

I crossed the room and wrapped my arms around him from behind. I hugged his back to my chest. "I'm sorry. You know I trust you. I should have told you."

Trevor turned around and hugged me to him. "Yeah, you should have."

I allowed myself to take strength from his embrace before taking a step back.

"Uh, guys," Mac said. "I'm glad this is all out in the open, but what are we going to do about all these photos?"

I shone my flashlight on the walls. It looked bad. Someone who knew I was Amanda had been stalking me for months.

"We have to call the police," Trevor said.

"No." I stopped him. "As odd as this sounds, I'm not supposed to tell anyone, not even the cops, that I'm really Amanda Parker. I'll call Donovan."

"Donovan?" Trevor asked.

"My handler. He'll know what to do."

"Are you in danger now? Do we need to hide you?" Trevor asked.

I shone my light on the wall and walked around in a circle. It appeared as if the photos had been posted in chronological order. There were photos of me when I lived in New York on one wall, and then others of me beginning maybe six months after that. The photos stopped at the point where Donovan had whisked Mom and me away and taken us to Madrona Island, and there weren't any photos that would have been taken since I returned. If the men I was running from had found me they must have left the area when I did. It didn't appear as if they'd returned, but that didn't mean they wouldn't.

"No," I finally answered. "I think I'm safe for now."

"Will you have to leave again?" Mac asked.

"Again?" Trevor asked, and then a light went on. "Your trip last spring. I take it you weren't visiting relatives in Minnesota like Mac told me."

"No, I wasn't visiting relatives. Donovan heard chatter that led him to believe the men who are looking for me had found me. He took Mom and me away while he explored the intel. It turned out to be inconclusive so we decided to come back. I guess the chatter he picked up was spot-on after all."

Trevor frowned. "You decided to come back. You might not have?"

I shook my head. "Donovan wanted to relocate us. I'm sure once he sees this that will be his plan once again."

"And we'd never see you again?"

"No. I'm afraid not. My own father doesn't even know where we are or who we've become. Once they erase your life they erase everything and everyone from it."

"We can't let that happen," Trevor said.

Suddenly I felt strong. "No. We can't."

Chapter 13

Tuesday, October 24

Donovan wanted to whisk me away as soon as he heard what I'd found. I refused. I was almost eighteen and old enough to take control of my own life, however brief the remainder of it might be. I'd talked it over with my mom and she'd agreed we should stay. There weren't any recent photos in the house and Donovan had sent a man from the nearest FBI office to tail me until he arrived and could manage the situation.

It was odd knowing the new senior who just happened to be in all my classes was really a fully armed FBI agent who went by the name of Chance and just happened to look young enough to pass for a high school student. I'd been instructed not to be overly chummy with him, but also not to do anything to let him lose me either. I knew the drill. I could do what I needed to do.

Spending time investigating Chelsea's stalker might seem like a meaningless activity in the grand scheme of things, but it gave me something other than the strangeness of my own situation to focus on. I planned to speak to Karina Hinton and Art Dupree today. If neither turned out to be Chelsea's stalker, and I didn't pick up any new suspects along the way, I was going to have to have a serious talk with Chelsea about bringing the adults in her life into the situation. The idea that the stalker might be the IT guy, Mike Walker, worried me more than just a tiny bit.

I knew Karina had history first period, so I waited in the hall for her class to let out. I could see my tail out of the corner of my eye, but obsessing about his presence wasn't going to change anything, so I tried to ignore him.

"Hey, Karina. Can I talk to you a minute?"

She looked at me for a second, as if trying to remember who I was and how she knew me. "Alyson, right?"

"Right." I couldn't use the article angle for this because Karina was on the newspaper staff, so instead I was pretending to be interested in photography. "I wanted to ask you about cameras. I know you do the photography for the school paper, so I was hoping you could help me out."

"Be happy to, but I have a class. If you want to walk with me, we can chat."

"Thank you. I appreciate it." I fell into step beside Karina. "What I'm most interested in is being able to take photos from a distance."

"How much of a distance?"

"Far. Like across a field or from down the street."

"You'll need a quality telephoto lens as well as a decent camera. The newer digital cameras will provide an autofocus feature, but to get really good shots you'll need to learn to manually adjust your settings. They have a good class at the community college, if you're interested. You'll need your own equipment, though; it isn't provided."

"What type of equipment do you have?" I asked.

"My camera is a fairly old Nikon I inherited from my dad. He also gave me a zoom lens with 800 magnification that's pretty awesome, but it's heavy and bulky. I'm hoping to get new equipment for graduation."

"I saw someone taking photos of the game last week from the hill across the field. Would your camera do that?"

"Sure. But I can't see that climbing all the way up that hill would provide an advantage. I took photos of the game from field level with a lens specifically manufactured to capture action shots of moving parts. Figuring out which lens is the best one to use, as well as which camera setting is best for each situation, is part of what that class will teach you. You should really look in to it."

"Thanks; I'll do that. One last thing on an unrelated topic: I know you work in the attendance office and I totally forgot my computer password. I don't suppose you can look it up for me?"

"Sorry. I forget mine every time I have to change it, so I feel your pain, but student aides don't have access to passwords. You'll have to ask Mr. Pruitt. You'll have to suffer through a ten-minute lecture on taking responsibility for your own password, but it's the only way. I even asked the principal if he could help me out the last time I forgot the sucker, but he said he didn't have access to the system without contacting the IT guy."

"Okay; thanks. I guess I'll suck it up and talk to Pruitt."

I was late to my next class, but I felt like the conversation I'd had with Karina was totally worth it. I was sure I could eliminate her from our suspect list; it didn't seem at all as if she was hiding anything, and she'd also answered my question about someone using the principal's access code to get into the system. At this point my main suspects were Art Dupree and Mike Walker. I supposed Mr. Pruitt could be a suspect as well because he did have access to everyone's passwords, but he didn't seem like the type and his name hadn't come up in any other context.

Despite the fact that I was dead tired after my ordeal the previous evening and just wanted to head to the library for a nap at lunch, I could see both Trevor and Mac were feeling a bit desperate about last night, so I promised to meet them in the lunchroom. I could see my tail was bored, bored, bored, but I didn't have a lot of control over these things, so I tried to go about my day the best I could.

"So, who's that hunkalicious guy watching your every move?" Chelsea asked as she slid onto the bench across the table from me.

"New guy," I answered without turning around.

"Have you met him? Can you introduce us?"

I took a spoonful of my yogurt. "I haven't met him, but he's in a couple of my classes, so I know his name is Chance. If you want to meet him why don't you waddle yourself over and say hi?"

"Waddle? I've never waddled in my life. And I will say hi, but first I want to find out where you are with that thing we can't talk about."

I glanced around the table. Mac and Trevor were listening intently and seemed amused by Chelsea's interest in the new guy, but no one else was playing any attention to us. "We've narrowed things down to two possible suspects at this point: Art Dupree and Mike Walker, the IT guy."

"Art didn't do it and I don't think Mike did either. I think you need to widen your search. There has to be someone else you haven't considered."

"We've been looking pretty hard."

"Well, look harder."

"I have a couple of people to talk to today, but if they don't pan out and I don't come up with any other suspects I'm going to insist you talk to your parents."

"You know I can't. They'd lock me in my room for safekeeping, completely destroying my social life. We've discussed this."

"I know we have, but if your stalker is an adult rather than a student, you could be in real danger. Heck, even if it's a student you could be in serious trouble. The only reason I haven't gone to your parents myself is because I think it most likely is one of the many people you've managed to piss off messing with you. Having said that, it might not be someone pulling a prank at all. Have you received any new photos?"

"None since the ones I showed you yesterday. Maybe whoever is doing this knows I'm on to them."

"Except you aren't."

"Maybe, but they might not know that. Everyone knows you like to stick your nose into everyone's business and people probably have seen you lurking around talking to people. Most of them probably won't have any idea what you're up to if you've stuck to our agreement, but the guilty party probably knows we're friends and may suspect we're on to them. The best thing that can happen as far as I'm concerned is if the lowlife just stops following me."

I scraped the bottom of my yogurt container and put the last bit in my mouth. "Maybe you're right and your stalker will just go away, but if you do receive any more photos remember to forward them to me."

Chelsea signed. "I'm a woman of my word and you're helping me, even though you don't have to, so I'll do what you say. In the meantime, I'm going to go see if the new hunk in school wants yours truly to give him a tour."

I had to suppress a chuckle. "Good luck with that."

"Boy, she's really something," Mac, who had thankfully held her tongue while Chelsea and I were talking, commented. "She could be in real danger and the only thing she's concerned about is how it might affect her social life."

"I can relate," I said.

Mac looked at me and frowned. "Yeah. I guess you can. Sorry."

"Let's just find the stalker and put this whole mystery to rest," I said. "I'm going to see if I can find Art. Once I speak to him we'll have eliminated all the student suspects, unless he turns out to be the guy."

"I'll take another look around during my internship to see if there's an angle we're missing," Mac volunteered. "We can meet up after school. I'd love to get an update on the other matter we can't discuss."

"I have practice," Trevor reminded us.

"Let's just meet at the field," Mac suggested. "We can chat and watch Trevor at the same time."

"Okay. My bodyguard and I will see you there after school."

I left the cafeteria and headed to the computer lab. I had a feeling antisocial and very uptight Art Dupree could be found either there or in the library. I'd spent a lot of time in the library lately and hadn't seen him there much, so I assumed the computer lab was his lunch time hangout of choice. Luckily, I was right and, even better, he was alone. I sat down at the computer next to his and logged on. I tried to look at the image on his screen without making it obvious I was doing so. It looked like he was writing code, most likely for a class he was taking.

"It looks like you really know what you're doing," I said as casually as possible.

"Yeah. I'm pretty good."

"Maybe you can help me. Someone hacked into my student account and sent emails that look like they're from me, but they aren't."

Art paused and looked at me. "Did you change your password?"

"I tried, but it seems that whoever broke into my account changed it, so when I log on the system asks me for my password, which I don't know. How am I supposed to change my password if I can't even get into the system?"

"I can get you in. Hang on."

I watched as Art's fingers flew over the keys. "Your name is Alyson Prescott and you have Harwin for homeroom, right?"

"Yes, that's right."

In less than two minutes, Art stopped typing. "Your password is Tucker." Art frowned. "It's odd that someone would hack your account, change your password, and then use the name of your dog."

"Tucker is the password I created," I admitted. "I guess I must have been doing something wrong when I tried before. That's so weird."

Art shrugged. "As long as you're in the system you should change your password anyway."

"I will."

Art punched some keys on the computer nearest to me, bringing up the page where passwords could be changed. He instructed me to choose a new password with both numbers and letters.

"How did you know my dog's name was Tucker?" I asked.

I noticed the FBI agent sitting at the very back of the room, paying close attention to our conversation. He didn't look very stealthy. He was staring right at us instead of looking at his own screen.

"I guess I must have overheard you talking about it."

I smiled. "Sure. That must be it." I frowned at the FBI guy, then returned my attention to Art. "So how did you get the password anyway? Are you that good a hacker?"

"I'm pretty good, but I didn't hack the system. My sister is dating the district IT guy and she happened to find out the password to the student file.

You won't say anything? Mike could get in trouble. I need you to keep this just between us."

I smiled even bigger, although I wanted to frown. "Sure." I did the silly blond hair flip thing and then said, "As long as you're in the system, can you help me find out who sent the email from my account? I'm really upset about the whole thing. Something like that can ruin friendships."

"Sure, I can probably help you. Who was the email sent to and when was it sent?"

I grimaced when I realized I didn't have an email for Art to inspect. "Oh shoot. I already deleted it."

Art shrugged. "Sorry. I'd need the email."

"You know, the same thing happened to Destiny Pilsner," I quickly improvised, remembering one of the emails sent to Chelsea. "Can we check her account? If we can trace her email we might be able to figure out who sent mine."

"Were the emails sent to the same person?" Art asked.

Chelsea was going to kill me, but I had to know what Art knew. "Yes. Chelsea Green. Destiny's account was used last week on Thursday."

Art logged into Destiny's account. It didn't take him long to pull up the right email. "It looks like Destiny logged into her own account using her own student ID and password."

"Yeah, but it wasn't Destiny. She told me so." I just hoped Art wouldn't check with Destiny; I'd never talked to her about the email and wasn't sure she even knew it was sent from her account.

"The email was sent from a computer here in the lab at twelve-twenty, which would be during lunch. I was in here on Thursday."

That grabbed my attention. "Do you remember who else was in here?"

Art paused. "I think it was just Mike and me. He was doing an update, and I've been working on a secret project during lunch every day for the past month. There must have been someone else in the lab I didn't notice."

Or, I realized, either Mike or Art was the stalker.

I thanked Art and left the room.

On one hand, Art could access the student passwords, so he could totally have sent the email; on the other, why would he tell me that he was alone in the room with Mike if he was the stalker? I also suspected he wouldn't have admitted he had the student passwords if he'd been using them to stalk Chelsea.

"Do you want me to take a look at the IT guy?" my tail asked as we walked down a deserted hallway.

"Would you?"

"I'd be happy to. It'll give me something to do while you're in class. I'll find a way to let you know what I find out."

Suddenly I realized that maybe having a gorgeous guy watching my every move would turn out to be a good thing after all.

Chapter 14

Mac was waiting when I arrived at the football field. I sat down next to her and my FBI tail headed toward the top row of the bleachers, where he pretended to be watching the guys go through their drills while messing around with his phone. I did feel bad he'd been stuck babysitting me. I was sure when he decided to join the FBI he'd had more exciting assignments in mind. I wasn't even sure what he'd been told about my situation. Probably not a lot. I supposed he was used to carrying out assignments with only minimal intel. I wasn't sure how long he'd been told to follow me, but obviously he couldn't tail me forever, which meant that decisions of some sort were going to need to be made sooner rather than later.

"So, any news about the creepy-photos-in-the-house situation?" Mac whispered.

"I know Donovan is looking in to things and trying to assess whether an immediate danger exists.

He sent some crime scene guys to gather the photos and take prints and feels fairly certain neither Mario nor Clay Bonatello have been in the house. He suspects they hired someone to track me down while they remain safely in hiding back in New York."

"I guess that's something."

"Yeah. I guess. I'm pretty sure there's no immediate danger, although I did feel like I was being watched last spring, just prior to Donovan whisking me away in the middle of the night. I suspect the photos were taken then. In fact, if you look at things like background images and the length of my hair, I feel certain the more recent photos were taken then."

"Did the guy who was sent to find you just leave after you disappeared?" Mac wondered.

"Probably. Although now that I'm back, it's most likely only a matter of time until he or someone else returns to finish what was started."

"Are you going to run again?"

I shrugged as a great sadness filled my soul. "I don't know. I don't want to have to run forever, but it isn't only me I have to consider. My mom gave up her marriage, her family, her career, pretty much her whole life, for me. I owe it to her to make good decisions."

"Is Donovan on his way to Cutter's Cove?"

"Not yet," I answered. "He's in New York, rattling some cages. He seems to think that putting pressure on the mob family might help flush Mario and Clay out of hiding. That's where they've been since the murder I witnessed, and Donovan has reason to believe the family isn't at all happy about all the attention their situation is bringing to them. Donovan's also hoping he can find the person they hired to take the photos and convince him to provide information on the brothers."

Mac crossed her arms over her knees and leaned forward just a bit. "Does Donovan know the identity of the person who took the photos?"

"As of the last time I spoke to him, no. The crime scene guys managed to pull some decent prints from the house, though. Donovan seemed to think it was only a matter of time until an identification was made. Once he has the ID he'll still need to track him down, but Donovan has a lot of resources at his disposal and he's very good at his job."

Mac glanced over her shoulder. "Is your tail with us for the long haul?"

"I don't know," I answered honestly. "My sense is that whatever's going to happen will be in the next few days. It's making me crazy that all I can do is wait to find out what my future will look like, but the reality is, waiting is all I can do. Which is why," I added, "I'm happy to have two other mysteries to occupy my mind."

"Okay, so where are we on the other two?"

I filled Mac in on my conversation with Art.

"Art has access to the student passwords?" she verified what I'd just told her.

"Yup."

"I find that disturbing."

"So do I. However, my overall impression was that he wasn't using the passwords for any sort of wrongdoing. He said he had a secret project he was working on, though he didn't go into detail. I suppose it could involve the use of student IDs. And he admitted to being one of only two people in the lab at the time the email Chelsea received on Thursday was sent."

"So it could be him," Mac said.

"It could. It seemed odd that he'd admit to having the passwords and to being in the computer lab when the email was sent if he'd done it, but he might have suspected what I was really up to and confessing to having the means to have sent the emails could have been his way to diminish my suspicion of him."

"So is he our number one suspect at this point?"

I shook my head. "He's still on the list, but not number one. My FBI buddy checked out the IT guy, Mike Walker. On the way over to the field, Chance informed me that Mike had a juvenile record that's been sealed. It would take a court order to unseal it, but Chance did some digging and found a school district report that said Walker was expelled from the high school he attended after he was accused of harassing two classmates. Walker finished his education at an online high school, then applied to college, where he studied technology. Chance didn't find any evidence that Walker had been in trouble with the law as an adult."

"So it sounds like Mike could be the guy," Mac stated.

"Maybe. The thing is, why would Mike be stalking Chelsea? According to Art, Mike is dating his sister. He has a decent job and probably makes decent money. Why would he risk that to follow Chelsea around? It makes no sense."

"She does have a way of putting people down and making them feel small. I'm not surprised someone would have an urge to mess with her."

"I agree, but I'm not convinced that someone is Mike Walker. Look at the time commitment involved. Whoever is stalking Chelsea has put a lot of hours into setting up those photos and waiting for the opportunity to catch her unaware. To me, that makes it seem as if Chelsea's stalker is obsessed with her. Mike spends a good deal of time on campus and could very well have met her here. It's even possible he could have become obsessed with her. But it seems like a long shot."

"So what now?" Mac asked.

"Chance and I discussed it, and the easiest way to eliminate Mike as a suspect is to determine whether he has an alibi for the time when one of the photos was either taken or sent."

"How do we do that?"

"I cut sixth period and took the time to create a timeline of when all the emails from the computers on campus were sent. All we need to do is get a look at Mike's work schedule and place him at another facility during the time one or more photos were sent."

Mac raised a brow. "You want me to hack into the school district employee files and find out where Mike was working on every day in question?"

"No. Chance will get the information."

Mac laughed. "Suddenly, I feel expendable."

"Don't. Chance has nothing to do while I'm in class. He sits in the back of the room and pretends to be participating, but he isn't. He's happy for something to do, and he has resources we don't."

"Yeah, I guess. I thought you said you weren't supposed to interact with him. It seems like you've been doing a lot of interacting."

"I'm not supposed to buddy up with him, but it would seem odd if we didn't chat if we're the only two people walking in a direction. Our interaction is supposed to seem natural and casual."

"I guess that makes sense. But if Mike doesn't turn out to be the stalker, who are we suspecting?"

I bit my lip. "I don't know. I guess we'll have to find a way to come at this from a different angle if Chance can prove Mike isn't the person we're looking for."

I glanced at the field, where the boys were doing sprints. Trevor wasn't only a talented quarterback but fast as well. I knew there were a handful of colleges courting him. Again, it made me sad that in less than a year Trevor would be going off to a college with an awesome athletic program and Mac would be heading to a college with a top-notch academic program, and I would be ... I had no idea where I'd be. What I did know was that our awesome trio was going to come to an end and there wasn't a single thing I could do about it. I supposed the loss of a high school gang was inevitable even if you weren't stuck in witness protection. And maybe it would be easier to deal with that reality if I felt like I was working toward my own glorious future instead of wondering if I'd even be alive in a year.

"What's on your mind?" Mac asked.

"Nothing."

"No, I think it's something. And judging by the scowl on your face, it's something unpleasant. Are you still thinking about Chelsea?"

"No. Not Chelsea."

"Then what?"

I looked at Mac. I knew my eyes would show the depth of my turmoil, but I didn't have the energy to mask it. "I was just thinking that regardless of what happens in terms of my witness protection, in less than a year, you and I and Trevor will be going our separate ways. I can't tell you how sad that makes me."

Mac reached over and hugged me. "I know. Me too. But it doesn't have to be that way. Trev and I have talked about trying to work it out to go to the same college. A lot of the schools he's looking at have fantastic academic programs as well as awesome football programs. I know you have a tough situation to deal with, but you reinvented yourself once before. You can do it again, only this time as a college student."

I shook my head. "Maybe, but they'd never allow me to go to the same college you and Trev attend. Whoever spent weeks photographing me last spring has to know we're besties. It would be too easy to track me down through you, which would put us all in danger. Let's face it: long-term relationships just aren't something I can consider."

Mac took a deep breath, held it for a moment, then let it out slowly. She took both of my hands in hers and looked me in the eye before she spoke. "I don't know what's going to happen, and I understand that the danger you're in is very real. I wish I could fix it for you, but I know I can't. What I do know is that as long as we're both alive, you'll always be in my life. No matter what happens we'll find a way. I love you. You're my best friend. And while Trevor needs some time to process everything, I know he feels the same way."

I could feel tears threatening, so I simply leaned forward and hugged Mac. She was right. Love would and should prevail. The Bonatello brothers had taken so much from me already. There was no way I was going to let them take the precious people I now had in my life.

My special moment with Mac was interrupted by the vibration of the phone in my pocket. I pulled it out and looked at the caller ID. "It's Woody."

"Then I guess you should answer," Mac said.

I hit the Answer button and put the phone to my ear. "Hey, what's up?"

"I have news. Actually, my news is that I don't have news."

"You called me to tell me that?"

Woody laughed. "Yeah, I guess that was lame. What I really wanted to tell you was that Eliston Weston had only the one sister who had a single child who has never traveled to the United States, and Eliston's wife didn't have any siblings. I checked three generations out, looking for male relatives that would have been the right age to have stayed with Mr. Weston during the time period the Moodys indicated and have come up totally empty."

"Maybe he was the son of a friend," I suggested.

"Maybe. But it'll be hard to verify without more information. I'm going to widen my search and speak to additional neighbors. I'll let you know what I find."

"Thank you; I appreciate that."

"I also wanted to let you know that the crime scene guys plan to release the house tomorrow morning, so you're free to use it for your event if you'd like. The deaths of the two victims occurred so long ago that there really wasn't any evidence to find. We still don't even know if they died in the house or were simply left there."

"And you still don't have causes of death?"

"Not so far. The skeletons are intact and don't seem to have been damaged, but the crime scene guys haven't found any viable tissue to run a tox screen, and the organs are completely decayed. They suspect the COD was something that wouldn't show up on skeletal remains, like a heart attack, poison, or suffocation. They haven't given up, but they're about out of ideas."

"Okay; thanks. Please do let me know if you come up with anything new."

I hung up and turned to Mac.

"Dead end?" Mac asked.

"Pretty much. They're releasing the house for the Hayride, which I know will make Caleb happy. I'm going to go back to the house before the crowd of volunteers arrive tomorrow. Maybe the ghosts can tell us what their remains can't."

"I'll go with you. I'm sure Trevor will too." Mac glanced behind her. "What about your tail?"

"He's just supposed to follow me around during the day. I guess they figure I'm safe in my own house at night because the security system Donovan installed before he left last spring rivals the one in the White House. Personally, I thought he went a bit overboard, but he wasn't all that comfortable letting Mom and me come back here, so we went with it. Anyway, you and Trev can come over and we'll sneak out after Chance leaves."

"Are you sure that's a good idea?"

"Not at all, but I need to help the boy move on. I sense his fear. I won't leave him there."

Mac took my hand in hers. "Okay. Let's figure this out. One way or another, we'll help the boy escape his earthly prison."

Chapter 15

Luckily, my tail left shortly after it got dark, so Mac, Trevor, and I were able to sneak out without too much trouble. Mom wasn't thrilled that I was going out, but she'd long since reconciled herself to the fact that I was an intelligent and resourceful person who was going to follow my heart. She agreed to keep Tucker occupied while we took Shadow along with us. We also agreed to check in by text every twenty minutes so she wouldn't worry.

Although the police planned to remove the yellow caution tape they hadn't done it yet, so we went through the woods and entered the house through the passageway. The boy was waiting by the entrance. I felt bad we hadn't visited the previous evening and wondered if he'd waited for us. I wasn't exactly certain ghosts experienced the passage of time; perhaps it hadn't mattered.

Shadow trotted directly to the boy, who bent down to hug the cat. I waited while the two reunited before asking the question I'd come to ask.

Eventually, I spoke. "We looked at the pads filled with the pictures you drew."

The boy shook his head.

"You didn't want us to look at them?"

He just looked at me.

"You didn't draw them?"

The boy shook his head again.

I paused to consider this development. "Okay. If you didn't draw the pictures can you show me who did?"

The boy started down the passage. Shadow trotted along behind and I followed them.

"I assume he's leading us somewhere?" Mac asked.

"It would seem."

"I hope it isn't to another body," Trevor added.

"Yeah, me too."

When we got to the point where the passage reached the house the boy disappeared through the wall. I tried the door handle, which, thankfully, no one had thought to lock, and we all squeezed through. The boy was waiting on the other side. When we were all in the cellar he started up the stairs and into the kitchen. Then he led us to the stairs leading to the second story. I was about to go up as well when the adult ghost appeared at the top of the stairs.

The ghost of the boy disappeared.

"Who are you?" I asked the adult ghost.

The ghost balled his fist and shook it in my direction.

"We aren't going to hurt you. We want to help you find peace."

The man started down the stairs, but I held my ground. He passed through me and I felt terror fill my soul. There was so much pain and anger tangled up with his essence. But there was something else too. Something primal. Something fierce and underdeveloped.

"It was you," I realized. I turned, but the man was gone. I could still feel his presence, so I continued to speak. "You drew the pictures on the pad."

He reappeared at the top of the stairs.

"Did you draw them when you were a child?"

The man disappeared through the wall behind him. I climbed the stairs and followed him. When I came to the room into which he'd disappeared I stopped to look around. The room was completely empty. I used my flashlight to carefully study every inch of the floor as well as all the walls. I felt in my gut there had to be a clue somewhere in this room, but I wasn't finding anything. If there ever had been anything here it was most likely long gone by now.

At the far end of the room was a closet that seemed out of place. I opened the door and looked inside. The ghost of the man appeared less than a foot in front of me. I screamed and jumped back, falling onto my backside.

"What is it?" Trevor asked, kneeling beside me.

I took several deep breaths and then answered. "The ghost of the man appeared in the closet. He startled me. I'm all right."

Trevor stood up, then lent me a hand. I took it and he pulled me to my feet.

"Maybe we should go," Mac suggested.

"No. We're close to our answers. I can feel it."

Mac continued to look more than a little worried.

"He can't hurt us," I assured my friends. "Startle, sure. But actually injure, I don't think so."

"What if he startled you while you were standing at the top of the stairs?" Mac asked. "You could have fallen."

I nodded. "Okay, you have a good point. I just need to be more careful."

Mac looked around the room. "Do you see him now?"

I looked around as well. "No."

"And the boy?" Trevor asked.

"Gone as well."

The three of us stood in silence. I had no idea what to do next. The room and closet were completely empty; still, I felt there was something we were meant to find.

I looked at Shadow, who trotted to the open closet and went inside. I followed him. I noticed Shadow was scratching at something in the corner and moved closer, shining my light on the spot. There was a metal handle attached to the wall. I turned it and a panel slid open.

"Well, I'll be. Another secret room."

I shone my light inside and then took a single step through the opening. It was a child's room, filled with childlike things. A model train, a set of blocks, and a table with crayons and pads filled with drawings.

"This must be where they kept the child before he died," I said aloud.

The man appeared. This time I didn't scream or jump back. I looked at him and suddenly I knew. The room didn't belong to the child but to the man with the mind of a child. I remembered the Moodys saying the teen who lived with Mr. Weston had mental issues.

"This was your room," I said.

The man floated over to the table with the pads. I remembered the drawings in the other one. They were so dark, filled with death and suffering. Immediately, I sensed that he was not only a child trapped in a man's body, but a soul filled with evil energy too.

"Who are you?" I asked again.

Woody had already eliminated the possibility of close relatives, and the only child Mr. Weston had was a son who'd died when he was nine. Suddenly I wondered if the ghost of the child could have been Weston's son.

But that made no sense. Mr. Weston's son had died before he moved to Cutter's Cove. Why would he bring the remains of his son with him? And the man ghost had obviously lived here, after Mr. Weston's wife and son had died.

Unless he hadn't.

"What are you thinking?" Mac asked.

"I don't think Mr. Weston's son died when he was nine. I don't think he died for another decade."

Mac frowned. "Huh?"

"The only thing that makes sense is that the ghost of the man was Mr. Weston's son. Mr. Weston knew he was dangerous, so he kept him locked up. At some point he must have died."

"Wait," Trevor said. "I thought Weston's wife committed suicide after the death of her son. If the son didn't die, that doesn't fit."

I paused to consider that. "What if the wife couldn't accept the fact that her son was a sociopath?

The drawings show terrible things. Decapitated animals, mutilated bodies, all sorts of horrific images, some of which may have been carried out. How would a parent deal with that? To know your son was the embodiment of evil without conscience?"

"Okay, I guess that makes sense," Mac said. "So Mr. Weston realized his son was a danger to others and locked him away. He told everyone his son had died. As a doctor, Mr. Weston would have been a respected man in the community, so chances are no one would have questioned him. His wife, however, couldn't deal with the situation and committed suicide. At some point Mr. Weston realized he needed a fresh start, so he moved to Cutter's Cove. He bought this huge house on a large piece of land where he could sequester his son. As the son grew he became smarter, more adept at escaping his confines. The Moodys saw him out and about, so Mr. Weston made up the story about a nephew. After the son died—and the boy who was staying with Mr. Weston was no longer seen in the area—it was assumed the nephew simply went home. Mr. Weston entombed his son in the secret room."

"That all makes sense," Trevor said, "but that doesn't explain who the child was or how the son died."

Trevor was right. We needed to figure out the rest of the story.

"What if Weston's son killed the child during one of the times he escaped? Like Frankenstein's monster?" Trevor asked.

"I guess it could have happened that way," I realized. "Mr. Weston knew what his son had done, but he didn't want him to spend the rest of his life in prison or a mental hospital, so he hid the body."

"Yeah, but if this monster killed the child you would think there would be all sorts of broken bones and there weren't any," Mac pointed out. "Besides, if a child was killed in the area someone would have noticed. There would have been a missing persons report."

"True," I responded.

The conversation paused as all three of us attempted to make sense of what we'd found. Neither ghost was visible, but I sensed that both still lingered. Shadow had wandered down the hall, and I went to find him. I checked every room on the second floor, then headed to the stairs that led to the attic. Shadow was standing at the door. I opened it and he trotted inside. Once inside the attic, I waited for Shadow to show me what he wanted me to find. He walked to a box and pawed at it. I set the box on the floor and looked inside.

"What is it?" Mac, who had followed with Trevor, asked.

"It looks like someone's personal possessions. I guess Mr. Weston's."

I began to remove items from the box. A dog-eared book. A pair of reading glasses. A couple of pens. A remote control. A notepad. A key. "It looks like the stuff you might have in a nightstand or maybe a chairside table," I commented.

"What does the key open?" Mac asked.

I picked it up and looked at it. "I'm not sure. It's small, so maybe a small lock of some sort. Or a trunk or safety deposit box." I looked around. There were stacks of boxes and some old furniture. I didn't see a trunk right off, but it was dark in the room and there was a lot of stuff packed in tightly.

"Let's get Caleb's generator-powered lights," I said. "Everything is in the room on the second floor. If the key opens a trunk of some sort maybe it's in here."

The three of us filed down the stairs while Shadow stayed behind. I could sense the spirits in the room and figured Shadow could as well. Caleb had shown me how to use the lights and the small generator, so we lugged everything upstairs. It took almost an hour to clear away enough of the boxes to find the chest. I used the key to open it. Inside were additional drawings, along with a metal box, which I opened to find a stack of envelopes.

"What did you find?" Mac asked.

I opened the first envelope, which contained the birth certificate of Mr. Weston's son. The second envelope contained a marriage license, the third a death certificate for his son when he was nine. The fourth envelope held the death certificate of his wife. I looked at each document, then passed it to Trevor, who passed it on to Mac.

Beneath the death certificate for his wife was a bill of sales for Weston's medical practice and his house in Kansas. The next envelope contained the deed to the house we were standing in, and beneath that, a newspaper article regarding a runaway, dated April 12, 1992.

"The boy in the box," I said aloud.

Mac took the article and read it. "So, if this runaway is the child in the box why didn't he show up on the missing persons reports Woody pulled?"

None of us answered right away.

"The boy went missing from a foster home two states away," Mac pointed out. "I don't think this could be the same kid."

"But what if it was?" I insisted. "What if the kid ran away and hopped a train or something and made his way to Oregon? What if he was camping out in the woods near this house and Weston's son found him? What if the son killed him? Once Weston realized what his son had done he would most likely have kept an ear out for missing kids. What if none were ever reported, so he simply left the body in his secret room?"

Trevor looked doubtful. "Seems like a long shot."

"There are two more envelopes," Mac pointed out. "Open them. Maybe one of them has the answers we still need."

The second to the last envelope contained a medical report that looked as if it might have been the results from a blood test. The final envelope contained a letter.

I read it aloud.

There are times in life when we are faced with impossible choices. We can become crippled by those choices, which can, at times, lead us to do things we would not otherwise have done. I was a doctor, a man who valued life and vowed to preserve it. I look back on the past few years and wonder how the man who stood so proud when he started his first medical practice evolved into the one writing what will serve as my final confession.

When my son was born I was filled with such joy. His future, I believed, was bursting with possibility, and I knew in my heart that he would one day do great things. As time passed, I saw my hope for his future decay into a terror I cannot quite explain. By the time he was four, I knew the child who was to be the light of my life was filled with a darkness I could never understand. With each year that passed, the darkness took over, and his actions became increasingly violent. My heart, once filled with happiness, became paralyzed with the fear that he would take the life of another.

Looking back, I realize I should have had him institutionalized, but he was still my son, and deep in my heart, I still loved him.

My poor, dear wife, God rest her soul, was terrified of him. So much so that she eventually took her own life to escape his dark presence. I knew at that moment I needed to make a change, so I sold my home and my practice and moved to the far-western shore of the country. I bought a large house that would serve as both my son's prison as well as my own, and I tried, to the best of my ability, to create a satisfying life for both of us.

It worked for a while. Julius seemed content to sit in his room and draw. But as he aged, the evil in him intensified, until eventually it engulfed him completely. He began to escape the prison I had created, but still I refused to send him away. I tightened the security each time he found his way into the world, but each effort on my part seemed to have minimal effect.

The day I found Julius with the child in his arms and realized my son had suffocated him, I knew I needed to end things once and for all. Julius would have suffered endless torture in an institution, so I fed him his favorite meal and laced his bedtime milk with a drug to make him sleep. Once he was out I administered the IV that slowly and peacefully ended his life.

I left both Julius and the child in a hidden room and waited for the authorities to come, but it never happened. After several months without a report of a missing child, I began to wonder. My own search turned up a runaway named Bobby Miller. He appeared to have the same characteristics as the boy Julius had killed, and I took some blood and ran a test. I was able to confirm with a fair degree of accuracy that the child in my secret room and Bobby Miller were one and the same. I considered calling in the authorities, but to what end? Bobby had been alone in the world and his killer was dead. I suppose I should answer for Julius's death, but rotting away in prison couldn't possibly relieve the pain in my soul. As of the time I pen this letter, I am unsure of my next move, but I felt I needed to let future generations know that true evil in its purest form does exist.

"Wow," Mac said when I had finished.

I handed the letter to Trevor. "Yeah, wow."

"What should we do?" Mac asked.

"We need to call Woody. This may mess up Caleb's plans for the Hayride, but I think our lost souls need to receive a proper burial if they're ever to find peace."

Chapter 16

Thursday, October 26

Woody took the information we provided and promised not only to confirm the identities of the two victims but to see that the remains of both Julius and Bobby received a proper burial. I hoped that would help both lost souls to move on. The thought of the man and the child being trapped in the house for all eternity was too sad to even consider. I thought I'd wait a day or two and then return to the house. If the ghosts were still in residence I'd know it, and if they had moved on, I felt I would know that as well.

I'd spent the previous day focusing on my homework. My FBI tail was still around, but I had a feeling his time with me was coming to an end. Donovan was trying to find a solution that would allow me to stay in Cutter's Cove, but as long as the

Bonatello brothers were alive, my life, and the lives of those around me, would be in danger.

Today, I decided, I would focus my energy on identifying Chelsea's stalker. She hadn't received any new photos since the ones from the previous weekend, but I knew I wouldn't feel right about things until I'd put this mystery to bed. I wasn't certain if I would even be attending Seacliff High the next week, and tomorrow was a half day, so today was when I'd have to find my answers.

Chance had verified that at least three of the days emails were sent from the high school, Mike Walker hadn't been on campus. Unless there were two or more people working together, he couldn't have been the stalker. The best lead we had was the single email sent from the attendance office computer. It seemed to provide a means of narrowing down the suspect field, but I also wondered why a student with the intelligence to obtain the student passwords in the first place would send an anonymous email from a computer with limited access.

The whole thing really didn't make any sense.

Maybe what I should be asking wasn't who'd had the means to send the emails but who'd had the motive to mess with Chelsea. She rubbed a lot of people the wrong way, but most of the students she pissed off wouldn't have spent the time to stalk her simply to make a point or exact revenge. As we'd concluded, for someone to want to stalk her, they'd need to be obsessed with her.

"Penny for your thoughts?" Mac asked, sitting down across from me at a table on the second floor of the library.

"I'm just trying to figure out who Chelsea's stalker might be."

"She said the emails and phone calls have stopped. Maybe you should just let it go. She seems to have."

I shrugged. "Yeah, I guess, but I hate to leave things unfinished. I'm not sure how much longer I'll be a student at Seacliff High and I want things wrapped up in case I need to leave."

A look of pain crossed Mac's face. "Don't even say that."

"Why not? It's true. I've spent a lot of time looking at the situation, and as much as it kills me to think of leaving, I can't risk my life and the life of those I love to protect my social life. That would make me no better than Chelsea."

Mac didn't reply, but I knew she agreed.

"If you ask me, the only one who would spend the amount of time the stalker has obsessing over Chelsea is Chelsea," Mac grumbled.

Mac had something there. If it was possible for Chelsea to take the photos of herself I'd definitely suspect her of making the whole thing up to get attention.

"Let's go over things again," I said. "We know whoever sent the emails had access to student passwords. As far as we know, the only people with that information are Mr. Pruitt, Mike Walker, Art Dupree, and maybe the principal."

"What about Art's sister?" Mac asked. "He told you he got the password that permitted him to access the student records from his sister."

"That's true. He also said she was dating Mike, so I'm assuming he was referring to an older sister."

"I can find out," Mac offered. She set her backpack on the table and pulled out her laptop. I waited while she booted it up. She typed in some commands that I suspected gave her access to school records. "Oh, wow."

I narrowed my gaze. "Oh, wow, what?"

Mac looked at me. "Art Dupree lives across the street from Chelsea."

I remembered the photo taken of Chelsea on Saturday morning. Of course. The stalker would have had to have been someone with easy access to Chelsea's house. It looked like we'd found our stalker, who, as it turned out, was the very first suspect I'd put on my list. I supposed that was a lesson in going with your first instinct.

"I bet he's in the computer lab. I'm going to talk to him," I said.

"Do you want me to come?" Mac asked.

"No, I think it will go better if I speak to him alone." I glanced at my tail. "Do me a favor and let Chance know what I'm doing and why I need him to give me some space. If he really feels the need, he can wait for me in the hallway outside the computer lab."

"Okay, I'll tell him. You don't think Art is dangerous, do you?"

I thought about the socially awkward guy. "No, I don't think so. And it isn't like I'm meeting with him alone in some isolated spot. I'm sure it'll be fine."

"Okay. Good luck."

Mac went to talk to Chance as I got up and made my way out of the library. I hurried across the campus and, as expected, found Art working on one of the computers in the computer lab. I sat down next to him, waiting to speak until he stopped typing.

"Are you having more problems with your account?" he asked.

"No. I appreciate your help, but I figured out who was sending the emails."

Art didn't reply.

"What I don't understand is why."

He looked down at his hands.

"You're a bright guy who seems to have a lot going for him. I don't understand why you would waste what had to amount to hours upon hours stalking someone like Chelsea Green."

Art looked up and turned to face me. "I've lived across the street from Chelsea since I was four. We used to be friends. Best friends. We even built a treehouse in my backyard where we used to hang out and escape from the world. I was never all that comfortable with other kids and Chelsea's friendship meant a lot to me."

I waited for Art to gather his thoughts. Eventually, he continued. "Then, when we were in the sixth grade, she got her braces off and began to climb the social ladder. She stopped coming around for quite a while. Of course, my feelings were hurt and I didn't understand how she could just throw away what we had. I struggled with her betrayal for quite a while, but eventually, I came to the point where I felt I could move on. And then her grandmother died. Chelsea was really close to her grandmother, and her death really affected her. She still wouldn't talk to me in public, but in the evenings, when none of her popular friends were around, she'd come over and we'd talk.

It wasn't the same as when we were kids, but it was something, and it meant a lot to me."

"And then…?"

"And then we started high school and suddenly, once again, I wasn't worthy of being in her orbit. She seemed to go out of her way to put distance between us. I guess at first I didn't care. She'd turned into a total snob and I certainly had better things to do with my time than listen to her prattle. Then, when we were sophomores, her best friend at the time started spreading rumors about her. Chelsea was devastated, and for the first time in almost two years she came over to my house just to talk. I was such a sucker, I immediately forgave all the mean things she'd done to me. We talked and I gave her advice, and we really seemed to be us once again."

"And then?"

"And then she made up with her friend and I was back to being the nerdy kid across the street who wasn't worthy of her attention. I was angry at first, but I got over it and moved on to other things. I would have gone on with my life and never given it a second thought if her parents hadn't hit a rough patch over the summer."

"Her parents split up?" I asked.

"Temporarily. They seemed to have worked it out, but during the period where they were fighting every day Chelsea began hanging out at my house the way she had when we were younger. Suddenly, we were back, and my world seemed complete. She apologized for the way she'd treated me and I really thought she cared about me. But as it turned out, she was just using me. The minute school started up, she was back to ignoring me. I was pretty devastated, but then I realized that, ever since we hit puberty, the only time she came to me was when she had a problem."

"So you created a problem."

"I guess it was lame, and I guess I wasn't thinking right, but yeah, that's the gist of it. I figured she'd be freaked out when she got the emails and come running to me to fix it, but instead of running to me, she ran to you. When you came into the lab the other day I realized you were close to figuring things out. I wanted to confess, but I suppose at my core I'm a coward. I did stop sending the emails, though, and I don't plan to send any more. Are you going to tell her it was me?"

I actually wasn't certain. "Why did you admit to having the student passwords? If you hadn't volunteered to help me I would never have known."

Art shrugged. "I guess there was some part of me that wanted you to figure it out. I hate being so needy. I hate that Chelsea has the power over me that she seems to. I guess I felt helpless to end it and hoped you would."

I had to admit I couldn't comprehend how someone would become obsessed with another person to the extent Art had become obsessed with Chelsea, but I'd also never been as socially awkward as Art seemed to be. I guess when social interaction is difficult you cling to those you feel the most comfortable with.

"I won't tell Chelsea it was you who sent the emails as long as you promise to stop. She seems to have moved on from the whole thing anyway. I can't claim to understand why you felt you had to do what you did, but, as I said, you're a smart guy with a bright future ahead of you. Don't ruin it by letting others define your values."

"I won't. And thanks."

The bell for fifth period rang and I said good-bye and headed to class. I wasn't sure what the future would bring, but at least I felt I'd tied up all the loose ends. If it was my destiny to leave Cutter's Cove I wouldn't have to feel I'd left unfinished business behind.

******

When I arrived home from school and saw Donovan's car in the drive my heart sank. I remembered what had happened the last time I came home to find my handler waiting for me. When Chance had told me after school that he'd been relieved from watchdog duty I should have realized the time of reckoning had arrived.

I knew I needed to go inside and face whatever was waiting for me, but my legs felt numb and I found I was unable to move. I picked up my phone and scrolled through the photos I had of Mac and Trevor. They meant the world to me. I really couldn't imagine my life without them. In that moment, I knew I would do anything to keep them in my life. I even understood why Art had done what he had.

I wiped the tears from my face and slowly opened the Jeep door. I climbed out and headed to the front door and the destiny that waited inside.

"Oh good, you're home." Mom hugged me the minute I walked inside. I could see she'd been crying, but she also had a smile on her face. I supposed she was trying to be brave for me. And I supposed I could be brave for her.

"What's going on?" I struggled to keep my emotions at bay as I prepared myself for the devastating announcement I knew was coming.

"Donovan's here. He has news."

I looked toward the living room "I figured."

I took one step and then another. I felt like a prisoner walking to her death. It felt like my heart was going to break into a million pieces, but I steeled myself to accept my fate like an adult.

"Donovan," I said as I stepped into the room. He had on a black suit and a white shirt that seemed much too formal for the occasion.

"Amanda. I'm glad you're finally home. Have a seat."

Odd that he should call me Amanda. He, of course, knew the truth but hadn't crossed the line between my two identities in the past.

I sat down and waited.

"We found the Bonatello brothers."

My heart skipped a beat. "You did? Are they here?"

Donovan shook his head. "No. Not here. They're dead."

I felt my breath catch. "Dead?"

"Executed. The popular opinion is that their sloppy murder of the men in the vacant lot and their pursuit of you brought more attention to the family than they were comfortable with. The family decided they were a liability and took care of them. We've unofficially been informed that the family has no beef with you."

I sat perfectly still. I wasn't sure what to think. "What does that mean?"

Donovan smiled. "It means you're free. The men who were after you are dead and the Bonatello family isn't interested in creating another problem by pursuing you. You can resume your life as Amanda Parker or you can remain here as Alyson Prescott. It's totally up to you."

I looked at my mom, who was standing in the doorway with tears streaming down her face. I had no idea what to say, so instead I started sobbing. There are no words to describe how it feels to have such a great burden lifted from your life. Mom crossed the room and I ran into her arms. I wasn't sure where my life would take me, but for the first time in a long time I felt like my life was finally mine to live.

Chapter 17

Saturday, October 28

Somehow Caleb had managed to work his magic and make the Hayride and haunted house a reality. I honestly had no idea how he pulled it off, but the house was completely decorated and the party was the best I'd ever attended. I'd been to the house a couple of times since learning the truth about the skeletons in the secret room and I was convinced beyond a shadow of a doubt that both ghosts had moved on. I felt good about the fact that I had helped the boy to escape the earthly prison that had entrapped him for so many years, and I even found myself hoping the man who had been filled with evil during his lifetime had finally found peace as well.

"I think your costume is a hit," I said to Mac, who really had rocked the whole zombie thing.

"Thanks. I think it turned out well. I'm sorry you didn't have time to come up with your own creepy outfit."

I shrugged. "I'm so happy and content at this point that I really didn't have it in me to do the whole gory thing. Maybe next year."

"We'll be in college next year," Mac said.

"True, but since you and I and Trev have decided to attend the same college I figure we can carry on the tradition in a new location."

Mac smiled. "I think that's a fantastic idea. Have you discussed the college thing with your mom?"

"I have, and now that the danger is gone she's fine with it. I hope we can find a place that will work for all of us that isn't too far away. I have a feeling I'm going to want to come home as often as possible. I haven't decided on a college, and I already miss Mom, Tucker, and Shadow more than I can hardly stand."

"Yeah. Me too. Oregon State has an excellent football program and a strong academic program, and it's close enough to go home for visits as often as we want. Trev and I have discussed it at length, while we're looking at a couple of others like Stanford, even it's a day's drive away. Suddenly I can't wait to see what the future holds."

I hugged Mac despite the pounds of makeup she was wearing. "It does feel like the world is shiny and new."

Books by Kathi Daley

Zoe Donovan Cozy Mystery:

Halloween Hijinks
The Trouble With Turkeys
Christmas Crazy
Cupid's Curse
Big Bunny Bump-off
Beach Blanket Barbie
Maui Madness
Derby Divas
Haunted Hamlet
Turkeys, Tuxes, and Tabbies
Christmas Cozy
Alaskan Alliance
Matrimony Meltdown
Soul Surrender
Heavenly Honeymoon
Hopscotch Homicide
Ghostly Graveyard
Santa Sleuth
Shamrock Shenanigans
Kitten Kaboodle
Costume Catastrophe
Candy Cane Caper
Holiday Hangover
Easter Escapade
Camp Carter
Trick or Treason
Reindeer Roundup – *December 2017*

Zimmerman Academy The New Normal
Ashton Falls Cozy Cookbook

Tj Jensen Paradise Lake Mysteries by Henery Press

Pumpkins in Paradise
Snowmen in Paradise
Bikinis in Paradise
Christmas in Paradise
Puppies in Paradise
Halloween in Paradise
Treasure in Paradise
Fireworks in Paradise – *October 2017*

Whales and Tails Cozy Mystery:

Romeow and Juliet
The Mad Catter
Grimm's Furry Tail
Much Ado About Felines
Legend of Tabby Hollow
Cat of Christmas Past
A Tale of Two Tabbies
The Great Catsby
Count Catula
The Cat of Christmas Present
A Winter's Tail
Taming of the Tabby
Frankencat
The Cat of Christmas Future – *November* 2017
The Cat of New Orleans – *February 2018*

Seacliff High Mystery:

The Secret
The Curse
The Relic
The Conspiracy
The Grudge
The Shadow
The Haunting

Sand and Sea Hawaiian Mystery:
Murder at Dolphin Bay
Murder at Sunrise Beach
Murder at the Witching Hour
Murder at Christmas
Murder at Turtle Cove
Murder at Water's Edge
Murder at Midnight – *October 2017*

Rescue Alaska Paranormal Mystery:
Finding Justice – *November 2017*

A Tess and Tilly Mystery:
The Christmas Letter – *December 2017*

Road to Christmas Romance:
Road to Christmas Past

Writers' Retreat Southern Mystery:
First Case
Second Look
Third Strike
Fourth Victim – *October 2017*

USA Today best-selling author Kathi Daley lives with her husband, kids, grandkids, and Bernese mountain dogs in beautiful Lake Tahoe. When she isn't writing, she likes to read (preferably at the beach or by the fire), cook (preferably something with chocolate or cheese), and garden (planting and planning, not weeding). She also enjoys spending time on the water when she's not hiking, biking, or snowshoeing the miles of desolate trails surrounding her home.

Kathi uses the mountain setting in which she lives, along with the animals (wild and domestic) that share her home, as inspiration for her cozy mysteries.

Kathi is a top 100 mystery writer for Amazon and won the 2014 award for both Best Cozy Mystery Author and Best Cozy Mystery Series.

She currently writes six series: Zoe Donovan Cozy Mysteries, Whales and Tails Island Mysteries, Sand and Sea Hawaiian Mysteries, Writers' Retreat Southern Mysteries, Tj Jensen Paradise Lake Mysteries, and Seacliff High Teen Mysteries.

Giveaway:

I do a giveaway for books, swag, and gift cards every week in my newsletter, *The Daley Weekly*
http://eepurl.com/NRPDf

Other links to check out:
Kathi Daley Blog – publishes each Friday
http://kathidaleyblog.com
Webpage – **www.kathidaley.com**
Facebook at Kathi Daley Books –
www.facebook.com/kathidaleybooks
Kathi Daley Teen –
www.facebook.com/kathidaleyteen
Kathi Daley Books Group Page –
https://www.facebook.com/groups/5695788231468 50/
E-mail – **kathidaley@kathidaley.com**
Goodreads –
https://www.goodreads.com/author/show/7278377. Kathi_Daley
Twitter at Kathi Daley@kathidaley –
https://twitter.com/kathidaley
Amazon Author Page –
https://www.amazon.com/author/kathidaley
BookBub –
https://www.bookbub.com/authors/kathi-daley
Pinterest – **http://www.pinterest.com/kathidaley/**

Made in the USA
San Bernardino, CA
30 August 2017